HER RIVER GOD WOLF

OBSESSED MATES BOOK 1

ARIANA HAWKES

D1608033

Imprint: Independently published

ISBN: 9798866250028

Cover art: Thunderface Design

www.arianahawkes.com

CONTENTS

Prologue   1
Chapter 1   7
Chapter 2   19
Chapter 3   35
Chapter 4   44
Chapter 5   57
Chapter 6   67
Chapter 7   79
Chapter 8   88
Chapter 9   98
Chapter 10   105
Chapter 11   116
Epilogue   125

Read the other books in the series   137
Read my Obsessed Mountain Mates series   139
Read the rest of my catalogue   141
My other matchmaking series   143
Connect with me   145
Get two free books   147
Reading guide to all of my books   149

PROLOGUE

"We're here." My mom's voice grates through the darkness of the car interior. She stamps on the brake and the car stops with an awful jolt that goes right through me.

The seatbelt crushes my boobs and adrenaline booms in my chest. "Where's here?" I squint through the windshield, but all I can see is midnight sky and dark, dark road.

"I've taken you as far as I can. Get out of the car, Vani."

"Please, mom—" I falter. The woman sitting beside me looks nothing like my mom. She's wearing a baseball cap, tugged down over her pale face. Her waist-length hair, which she usually wears loose like all the women on the territory, is twisted into a braid and tucked down the back of her jacket. She's also wearing pants for the first time in my life.

"Please, what?" Her jaw is set, lips drawn into a grim line.

Stay with me? Pull out a secret wad of cash you've been squirrelling away for years and take us both someplace safe?

I lean over, try to hug her, but she winces and pulls away. Nothing new there. She's never given me a scrap of affection.

"Just go. Get out of here."

My throat feels like it's closing up. "C-can you give me our address?" I choke out. Twenty-two years old and I don't know my own address. I don't know a lot about the outside world, but I understand that's damn weird.

"You won't need it. Just go."

I stare into the darkness and a pathetic whimper breaks from my throat.

"Vani, I need to get back, goddamnit!" Her eyes are wild, teeth bared.

My heart lurches. She's right. Every second I delay, I put her in more danger. I'm lucky she brought me this far. "Okay, I'm going." My hand goes to my belt and I unfasten it with trembling fingers.

Inside the car, I cling to the vestiges of my own world—my mom. That familiar, slightly bitter smell of hers. The smell of sadness and disappointment, I used to think. Outside is the raw unknown. If I open the car door, I'll slash that world right open. And the thought of what might lie within it paralyzes me with terror.

"You'll be fine, Vani. You're tougher than me." Her voice is a shade softer, but then it hardens again.

"Just don't give your heart away to a man."

A wave of nausea washes through me. This was what brought me here. My failed mating.

The humiliation.

The ugly consequences spilling out from it. This manic night-time drive through miles upon miles of deserted roads, to some place my mom claimed had been passed on to her by the angels.

"Mom—" My throat closes convulsively. I want to tell her I'll miss her. I'll think of her. But she's banned me from uttering words of affection. *Pretty words don't belong in pack law*, she's told me, ever since I was a tiny pup.

"I'm not your mother."

"W-what do you mean?" I choke out, and another whimper breaks loose. I know it will disgust her, but I can't hold it back.

"I just raised you. That's all." Her voice is savage now. Vengeful.

I gasp, a shard of pure agony stabbing me in the heart. If a tree crashed through the windscreen right now and a branch pierced my chest, I don't think it could've hurt any more than this.

She leans across and I think she's going to hug me after all, but she yanks the lever and shoves the door open. The rusted, warped door creaks loudly. Cold air blows in, bringing a night full of unfamiliar smells.

Violent shivering takes hold of me, but I haul myself out in a daze, those brutal words hijacking every rational thought. I pull my backpack onto my shoulders, and fumble with the door until I succeed at closing it.

Immediately, my mom hits the gas and hauls the car into a U-turn. Her face is tight and pallid against the darkened interior, and she doesn't acknowledge me as she squeals off.

Out of my life for good.

I watch the car's red taillights until the night swallows them up, along with everything I know.

I bite down on my thumb to stop myself from breaking out into sobs. And I wonder if I imagined those grimy trails streaking her cheeks.

I START WALKING along the road, with no idea where I'm going. My night vision is sharp, but before long, I'm blinded by tears.

Not my mother?

I don't know what's worse—having a mother who doesn't love me, or realizing she didn't love me because she wasn't even my mother.

It's hard to breathe, as if there's a band tightening itself around my chest, and I turn clumsy, uncoordinated. I stumble on the hard road surface. Nothing but darkness all around. I trudge for I don't know how long. Miles maybe, my feet plodding and slow. Blacktop, grass verge and starless sky. My backpack, containing my every possession, is light compared to the all-consuming ache in my insides.

I'm so tired. My feet ache like crazy and, despite the fear charging my veins, I let off epic yawns, one after another.

At last, the highway ends. There's a soft rushing sound and the sharp smell of river water. I head toward it, soothed by the signs of nature.

I come to an old wooden bridge. Maybe I can shelter underneath it for the night. But the bank is hella muddy,

I realize too late. My left foot slips, then my right, and suddenly I'm tumbling, all the way down the steep bank. I panic as the water rushes up to meet me. I'm not a good swimmer.

Then a patch of mud breaks my fall. Thick, stinking river mud.

It sucks at my feet and I feel like it wants me. Wants to draw me into its dark embrace.

I know I should fight it.

But I'm too exhausted and sad.

Instead, I scramble under the bridge and curl up.

Waiting for whatever might come.

1

Beau

*E*very morning, a half hour before sunrise, when the sky is still dim and dawn is an orange strip on the horizon, is the time when I rouse my ass from my bed. Let my animal do the things it was designed to, without fear of scaring the hell out of the human race.

I bound out of bed, having slept deeply as always. The peaceful sleep of the untroubled mind, as I like to say. I yank open the door of my motorhome and inhale. The sweet morning breeze fills my lungs, wafting in a feeling of hopefulness with it. Not that I need to hope for anything. I've got everything I need right here, in my little mobile lair.

The abandoned supermarket parking lot where I've been holed up for the past couple of weeks is still shrouded in darkness, and there's not another soul around. Just the way I like it.

I flick on my coffee machine, so my home will be full of the rich scent of java when I return, and I charge out into the breaking day.

No need for clothes as I stride to the river that runs alongside the lot. The grassy bank is soft and dewy beneath my bare feet. There's a good spot where I can plunge right in without cracking my head open, and I take advantage, hurling myself into a dive. I slice clean through the water, slick as a fish, and the river receives me like one of its own.

I like to wash up first. I scrub myself all over, chasing away the shadows of the night. Beautiful freshwater rushes around me in this unassuming piece of paradise.

I'm a free spirit, living, travelling as the mood takes me. Looking for paradise wherever I find it.

Does it get lonely sometimes? people ask me.

Hell, yeah, it does. But I've seen its evil twin. I've stared into the abyss of hostile fate, nursed the bitter seed of a broken heart, and it's been enough for one life-time. I'm a lone wolf. It wasn't the destiny I was raised for; I had blood of the alpha line running in my veins. But I had to leave my pack, before my beast destroyed everyone I cared about.

Fifteen years alone, and I'm happy like this.

When I'm done getting clean, I take on my animal form. My wolf springs out of me, fast and eager. It's more accustomed to running, of course. And at dusk, I'll ride my motorcycle to a forest a few miles away, run for an hour. But while I'm staying by the river, I take advantage of this delicious, cool water, and I let my beast explore its amphibious side.

With long, fast strokes, I swim upstream, scattering shoals of silvery fish. From time to time, I snap one up in my jaws. Not my favorite cuisine, but they make a convenient breakfast. Perhaps I was a bear shifter in a previous life.

If I keep going, I'll pass a bunch of bridges. I set myself a challenge; I'll aim for the fifth one along, before I'll turn and let the current carry me back home.

But when I pass the first one, something catches my eye.

A bunch of rags stuffed into the hollow between the underside of the bridge and the narrow river bank. Strange. That wasn't there yesterday. I swim closer. No, not rags—a person. I can't see a face though—it's hidden by a hoodie and their folded arms.

I edge closer still, and my wolf's nose twitches: female, young.

My ears tune in. I hear the regular breathing of deep sleep. She doesn't seem to be hurt. Homeless? A runaway? *Poor thing*. I'll leave her be, check on her on the home stretch, I tell myself. She seems comfortable where she is. No point disturbing her.

I turn to go—or at least, I try to, because my wolf is refusing to budge. Ears pricked up, gaze fixated. Every nerve focused on this snoozing bundle.

Then the bundle stirs.

A patch of dewy cheek emerges from the folds of fabric and a little whimper comes with it. A terrible expression of distress and loneliness. It slices right through me.

And I know there's no way I'm going anywhere.

In a flash, I shift. My wolf fights me hard as I fold it back inside my human form. Its prickly fur pushes right up beneath my skin, paws scrabbling, panting in anticipation. Why the hell is it so riled up?

My feet find purchase on the slippery stones, and I start to wade toward her—

And then I remember that I'm buck naked. Humans freak out at shit like that. I'll probably scare the heck out of her. Clothing definitely not optional.

I sprint flat out to my vehicle, and I'm back in less than minute, T-shirt and shorts clinging to my wet form like a second skin. Not a whole lot different from being naked, but at least I'm not about to get arrested for indecent exposure.

It's hard to approach the girl, since there's a ton of mud all around her, so I jump back in the river, wade up close again.

"Ma'am?" I call, making my voice human-gentle. "Ma'am, are you alright?"

The pile of fabric shifts around. More pale skin emerges.

And then a pair of eyes flash, blinding me like full-beam headlights.

I swear I almost fall back and go right under.

Not some teenage runaway, but an adult woman.

With the clearest lake-green eyes I've ever seen. Fresh apples, sun-dappled forests. Sweet garden of paradise. But cut-glass sharp. Capable of slaying a man.

They're fringed with thick lashes, and they peer out from beneath long, dark bangs. As I watch, awestruck, a snub nose appears, scattered with freckles, and a pair of cherry-shaped, pink lips.

She's the prettiest thing I've ever seen. And she smells like something sweet and soft. Something that hasn't come into its own yet.

Then her eyes blaze double-strength and her lips draw back, showing sharp white teeth.

Feral.

Wolf.

The realization rocks me on my feet. Her scent is weak; that's why I didn't pick up on it right away. But it's unmistakable. Her animal is there, somewhere inside of her.

My wolf inhales hard and her scent fills my lungs like a drug. Sweet euphoria blows in.

Intoxicating.

Then it utters the word I hoped I'd never hear again in my life:

Mine.

My body jerks, and just like that, I want to run. Get the hell away from this feral goddess.

My wolf howls and the sickness threatens.

All these years…

All these years I've spent avoiding females. Happy in my own company. Never mating. Not even one-nighters. Keeping my wolf calm. Denying its impulses. Trying to make it *forget*.

And now it comes and finds me, on this peaceful riverbank. A stab of fate. Bringing the whole sky down with it. Dragging me under.

I need to get away from her. She's fine. Health glows from her pores. She looks like she's capable of taking care of herself. I don't need to make her my problem.

Time jolts forward. And I remember I'm not an asshole. I've scared this girl, and that was worse than not waking her at all. I can't leave her like this.

"I'm not going to hurt you," I say. A dumb comment for sure, but my brain is too paralyzed for anything more nuanced.

Those bottle-green eyes fix on mine with hostility.

I swallow hard, clear my throat. "I was just going for my morning swim, like I do every day. And I saw you sleeping there. Thought you might be in trouble."

She blinks, emotions clouding behind her eyes. But still she says nothing.

I work my jaw back and forth. Maybe she's non-verbal. "You speak?"

"Yes." She nods fiercely.

"You're safe with me, little wolf."

"Wolf? How did you know?" Her voice is surprisingly strong. There's something in it, a kind of catch. Like a foreign accent, but not.

I gesture at my body, and her gaze follows the movement of my hands, leaving a trail of fire in its wake.

"You're a wolf, too?" She wrinkles her nose and it's kind of adorable.

"Yup. Beau Matherson. Investigator, sometime bounty hunter. Werewolf." I tilt my head toward her in a mock bow, and a ghost of a smile tugs at her lips.

"Now, you gonna tell me what you were doing, sleeping down here in all this mud, like a river rat?"

This seems to bring her to her senses. She unfurls from her nest, then she clambers awkwardly to her feet, bracing her hands on anything that isn't mud. I help her, advising her where to grab onto for support.

She draws herself up to her full height. And my breath shudders in my throat. She's filthy. Absolutely caked in stinking river mud from head to toe. She's wearing some frumpy old clothes that look like she pulled them out of a thrift store's reject bin, and her hair is matted, so coated in filth I can't even tell what color it's supposed to be. But beneath all that is a knockout body. All lush, womanly curves.

Beauty glows from her, like a firefly in a storm.

My wolf whines its approval.

Fuck. She could annihilate me.

"I was walking, and I fell," she says.

I wait, expectantly, but she stays silent.

"You have a home to go to?"

Her face freezes, then it starts to crumple. She sets her jaw and shakes her head fast.

"None at all?" I blow my cheeks out.

Well, shit.

"You are over eighteen?" I scan her face. Hard to guess her age with all that mud.

"Twenty-two," she mumbles.

Good.

"How about we get you back to my place, get you cleaned up, then figure out what we're going to do next?"

She gnaws on her pretty lower lip, and her eyes dart sideways, like what she wants to do right now is run.

"If you're gonna bolt, best to do it in a clean set of clothes." I point at my vehicle, barely a speck in the distance. "That's my place."

Her emerald eyes narrow as she takes it in. "You live in a...a bus?"

"Yup. Fully plumbed in. You can take a hot shower."

She looks down at her clothes, and finally seems to absorb just how filthy she is.

"Okay, thanks," she says, and flashes a little smile.

It goes all the way to her eyes, and I'm damned if it doesn't light me up like a jack-o'-lantern. Next thing I know, I'm grinning like an idiot at the thought of having this little ragamuffin getting mud all over my bathroom.

I pull myself up the steep bank, covering myself in mud in the process, then I reach for her backpack, which is also filthy and wet.

"Oh—" she says, like she just remembered it, and the word is so laden with sorrow, I feel it in my own soul.

I'll find out what she's suffered, I vow. Just as soon as I've gained her trust. Then I'll hunt down whoever's hurt her, and I'll tear them apart.

I try to carry her bag for her, but she snatches it back and grips it fiercely against her chest.

I shouldn't like that show of feistiness so much.

WE WALK TO MY RV, and I have to go slower than usual, shorten my typical lope so I don't get ahead of her. She's short, barely comes up to my shoulder, and I try not to think that's a perfect height for her to lay her head on my chest.

As we arrive, I tear off my drenched T-shirt and wring it out irritably. Damned thing feels like it's trying to suffocate me.

"Home sweet home," I say, hoping my corniness will relax her a little. But when I turn to her, she's staring at me, transfixed. Her eyes drag up and down my body, and they turn dark, stormy. At the same time, her sweet cherry lips part.

She likes what she sees.

Holy shit. A deep growl rolls through my chest.

Energy crackles in the air. An electrical storm, flying from me to her, and back again. Momentarily, I glimpse her wolf—something silvery and soft, rising to the surface and falling away again, quick as a fish.

My own wolf pants.

Mate.

Mine.

I turn away quick, the sickness lurching through me again. This is getting worse by the second.

Not my mate.

I have no mate.

Silently, I repeat the words, until the beast retreats.

Then I turn back to her.

"You can put your bag down." I point to the table and chairs I've got set up under my slide-out awning. Not that anyone ever sits in the chairs but me. "You got anything to wear in there?"

"Uh—" she dumps the bag on the table and starts

rooting through. A bunch of things emerge, all drenched. She holds up some kind of tight black pants. Legging, I think women call them. They're mostly unscathed. She rolls them up with a couple of smaller bits of fabric.

Underwear. I bite back the thought, but it's too late. My wolf is already racing ahead, picturing her in a bra and panties. In no underwear at all. My cock swells beneath the zipper of my shorts, which are currently clinging to me like a second skin.

Too much. Too fast.

I exhale slowly, think of ugly, tragic things until my erection recedes.

"I can lend you a shirt?" I offer.

She nods. "Thanks." She looks a little softer now. Like she might be starting to trust me, just a little.

"Let me show you around inside—" I start to say, then I remember how I left my bed still made up, the sheets no doubt tumbled across the mattress. "On second thoughts, you take a look inside. I'll wait out here. Guess it's not appropriate for, you know—"

I cough, don't finish that thought.

Not appropriate, or safe for a guy to be alone in a small space with his mate. Who he hasn't claimed.

"On third thoughts, let me get your shower stuff all set up." I dive through the door of my RV, grateful for a moment to force my desire—my wolf—back under control.

My bathroom is small, but it's functional. I can't always bathe in rivers, and I'm not a wolf who likes to skip personal hygiene. I check the water tank, which is almost full, and turn on the boiler so the water will run nice and hot. God knows this poor girl deserves a little comfort. Then I grab a brand-new bar of soap out of my supplies and add it to the shampoo on the shower shelf. My towels are kinda basic, probably what's known as guy's towels, but I pick the softest one I have and hang it on the hook on the bathroom door. Then I gaze at my meagre toiletry collection in dismay. There's a toothbrush and toothpaste. I trim my beard with scissors from time to time. Even though my hair's longish, it does its own thing and it doesn't need combing. I sure hope she has her own washbag.

Lastly, I fold the bed back into its alcove, and some of the tension leaves my body.

When I come back outside, she's sitting at the table, leafing through a notebook. Her shoulders are hunched, and so vulnerable they slay me. I want to protect this girl from anything that could hurt her.

At the sound of my approach, she snaps the notebook shut and stuffs it in her bag. As she looks up, her forehead is furrowed in sadness. If she was mine, I'd draw all that sadness out of her, then I'd kiss it away.

Instead, I gesture at the open door. "All yours," I tell her.

She leaps up and scurries inside, and I appreciate just how uncomfortable she was in those clothes. She's taken the backpack with her. It's going to leave a ton of mud in the RV, but I get it. It's probably the only thing she owns in this whole world.

She's also left a trail of mud on the table, the chair

and all the way up the steps. A surge of tenderness burns through me.

I keep myself busy, cleaning up, trying not to listen for her.

But it's no good. The boiler hisses as the shower turns on, and my whole being turns to molten lava. This curvy little she-wolf, all naked in my lair.

It's more than a lone wolf like me can take.

2

Savannah

I shouldn't be here, in this stranger's home, I think as I stand under the shower, scrubbing at my skin. The hot water draws the cold out of my bones, but the black mud is stubborn, clinging, and my mother's dark warnings flood back to me. He could jump in the driver's seat right now and drive me off someplace. Abduct me. Do anything he likes with me. There's no one to look out for me, to wonder where I've got to. Unease prickles in my stomach as I wonder if I've just done something real dumb. Something even worse than being rejected and abandoned.

But it doesn't *feel* like that.

As I watch the mud pour down the drain, I have the weird sense that it's my old life draining away from me.

I have no reason to trust Beau, except it felt like he was supposed to find me here.

Last night, when I skidded down that riverbank, I thought I'd tumbled into the mouth of hell. The blackness had risen up to receive me. To swallow me whole. I don't remember falling asleep, but awful nightmares terrified me all night long. I dreamed that I was already dead, sunk down to the river bed, tangled up in the weeds and stones.

And this morning, Beau Matherson brought me back to life. I was like a primordial creature wallowing in the mud, and he dragged me out and gave me a second chance.

His voice—a low, vibrating growl. A powerful voice made soft. It broke right through my nightmares. I opened my eyes and saw a sight I know I'll never forget:

A river god. A massive, broad-shouldered man, towering over me, water droplets glistening on him like gold dust. His clothes all soaked and clinging to him. Dark, wet hair hanging in his eyes.

And what eyes. As true as the brightest sky, burning through the darkness. Burning with worry for me.

As he took me in, he rubbed at his short beard, scattering more golden droplets, and my heart flipped. No one has ever worried about me before, in my whole life.

That's not me feeling sorry for myself. That's just how it is. Life was hard on the territory. If you don't look out for yourself, no one else is going to.

And when those burning-sky irises locked onto mine, I thought, *reborn*.

I was being reborn right here.

Just now, I wrote the word in my journal, and it seared through the pages.

He might have come to hurt me, to do those awful things my mom had warned me about. But when he lifted me up from the bank and led me here so gently— like I was a horse and he was afraid I was going to bolt —he felt like my savior.

Then he stripped off his shirt. His glorious body cast in gold by the morning light. Muscles like a river of boulders, tattoos adorning him like blessings.

When I look at him, I can't breathe. Dizziness trembles through me, and little sparks of fire light all over my body.

I want to stare at him all day long. I want to press my mouth to his skin. Feel its velvet, inhale his warmth.

I've never felt like this before, never desired another person before.

Frigid.

That's what they called me. That's why I was rejected—that and the fact I couldn't shift. That ugly moment seared into my mind for eternity.

Stripped bare, my body on display to the whole pack, for the first time since I was a little cub. And my intended, an alpha-in-waiting, walking around me in a circle.

Sniffing me.

He said I didn't smell right. That I had no scent.

Everybody laughed at me.

Then he told me to shift. I've never shifted before. My mom told me it would happen when I met my mate, but it didn't happen with him. I tried and tried till I hurt all over, and he laughed his ass off at me, and everyone else joined in, calling me names.

Frigid bitch.

What do you expect from a halfling?

I wasn't a real wolf and they knew it. Too soft, too chubby, and I didn't smell right.

He said he didn't want me in his harem.

My mom had warned me what my mating ritual would be like and I'd been dreading it for months. But I couldn't even be relieved it wasn't going to happen, because he warned me there would be consequences. *No room in my harem for a frigid female. We'll sell you to another pack.*

I think he took it as a personal slight that I didn't get aroused by him, and he wanted to punish me.

A part of me shut down, right there; a part that had never had a chance. A bud killed by frost. Mating, pups. The whole thing. It wasn't for me. I was as confused as hell. I'd never wanted this life for myself. But now I was being told I wasn't good enough for it, it hurt like crazy.

That's why my mom helped me escape—no, not my mom, apparently. But I'm not sure what else to call her. Not that it matters. I'll never see her again. The woman who raised me without loving me.

We learned that I was going to be offered to a pack of vicious half-breeds. All kinds of weird species, united in their bitterness, because some of them couldn't shift, or they could only shift half-way, and they'd gotten stuck like that.

She stole a car, and we drove overnight to Perdue Town—a place she'd heard was full of waifs and strays.

She wouldn't tell me how she knew about it. Just said it was the best place for me. She risked a lot bringing me here, and I'll always be grateful to her for that.

Last night I thought she'd lied. That she'd delivered me to hell instead. But here I am, in the little home of a big wolf man whose eyes tell me he's going to save me.

As I run my soapy hands over my body, I imagine it's his touch. Gold dust tingles on my skin. Rivers of gold flow in my veins.

Beau Matherson makes me feel hot and soft and achy in a way that tells me he's the only one who can fix it.

But that can never happen. When he finds out I'm a wolf without a scent, he'll reject me. And already I can't stand to see his eyes go dim with disappointment.

I'm a frigid female. Not fit for anyone's harem.

I could stay under this blissful hot water for hours, but I go as fast as I can, guessing the tank is small. When I'm sure there's no more mud, I finish rinsing my hair and step out of the shower. I towel off and get dressed. Thank goodness my clean underwear stayed dry, and the leggings, too. But as for the shirt Beau has put out for me... I button it up and it goes all the way down to my knees. It's blue plaid and very soft. I roll the sleeves up to my elbows and try to smooth it down, so it looks more like a dress.

There's no mirror in the bathroom and just as well, as I don't want to see how ridiculous I look right now. Actually, I don't care so much. Because I kind of like wearing Beau's shirt. It smells freshly laundered, but I wish it smelled of him. I rub the collar against my cheek and I imagine how it usually rides against his strong neck, the hairs of his beard catching against it. I'd like to feel his beard chafing my skin, I think, and the thought wafts another breath of gold dust through my soul.

When I emerge from the bathroom, there's an incredible smell of cooking coming from the other side of the bus. Beau is not in the tiny galley kitchen, though. My mouth waters and I remember I haven't eaten for at least a day.

I hop down the three steps to the outside and dump my dirty clothes in a heap on the ground.

And my breath catches at the sight of him.

Beau is arranging something on the table. He's got his back to me, a fresh white T-shirt pulled tight across his big shoulders. Deeply tanned arms setting off the dazzling white.

And then he turns, like his ears were pricked up. Waiting for me.

What an arrogant thought. My cheeks warm.

He looks me up and down and his chest rises and falls.

I go still. I know I look ridiculous, but suddenly I can't stand to be humiliated again.

Can't stand for this gorgeous man to laugh at me. I think my stupid heart would shatter to pieces, all over the parking lot.

He takes a step closer, and his lips part.

My heart pounds and my ears ring, bracing themselves for a sentence I'll never forget.

"Well now, don't you look—" Those sparkling eyes

turn stormy, and the tip of his tongue runs along his upper lip thoughtfully.

And now my heart hammers even harder because I realize he's not amused by me. No, there's something else in the gaze that's raking me from head to foot.

My eyes cling to the sight of his tongue sliding along his full, firm lips, and a shiver blasts through me. It prickles all over my skin, before alighting on my nipples.

What the hell?

For the first time in my life, I'm aware of my nipples. They're no longer sitting quietly behind my bra; they've turned to aching, burning points. I fight the urge to feel at them. Instead, I risk a quick look. Yup, there they are, poking through the soft fabric of Beau's shirt.

When I raise my head again, I see Beau has zeroed in on them, too. And I hear his breath coming heavy and rough.

I picture his dark head bent to my breasts, gently sucking them, one then the other. My hands tangling in his hair, my nose full of his scent.

Now the apex of my thighs starts to tingle as well.

Well, this is awkward.

"—refreshed," he says.

"Huh?"

"You look refreshed from your shower."

"Oh." I'm stupidly disappointed.

I fuss with my bangs. My wet hair is clinging to my face. "I must look a sight."

He shakes his head. "Not at all. You a redhead?"

"Kinda. More black than red, I guess." I force my fidgeting hands down by my sides.

"Bare feet…so tiny," he says wonderingly. "They shouldn't be bare on the parking lot though. You might step on something sharp. Broken glass or worse."

"They're stronger than they look." I try to sound offhand, but his scrutiny is making me a little panicky. It's not that I don't like it. I'm just not… used to it.

"Thanks for the shower."

He breaks into a grin as if he's relieved by the change of topic, too. "You're very welcome." He gestures to the table. "Let's eat now."

Belatedly, I notice that the table is stacked with a ton of food. Sausages, bacon, eggs, toast. Beau was cooking up a storm while I was getting clean.

I slide into my seat and stare at my heaped plate. "This…this is all for me?"

He gives a deep, throaty laugh. It's a nice sound, and I think how I'd like to hear it some more. "Girl, I can hear your stomach rumbling from here. Dig in."

So, I do. Things like this were rare treats on the territory. Most of the time, me and the other non-shifting species were lucky if we got fresh meat at all.

I feel like I'm eating like a beast, but I can't help myself. I'm so damn ravenous. After *that* awful humiliation and rejection, I lost my appetite and didn't eat for days. But looks like it's returned with a vengeance. I don't look up until I'm done, and then it's with a flood of embarrassment.

Beau has cleared his own plate and he's watching me with kind eyes.

"What happened, girlie?" he says.

I take a deep, in-out breath.

"My pack... I had to leave... my mom. She's not—" I break off with a sob, bury my face in my hands as the last few days hurtle back to me.

"Hush, everything's going to be okay now." He takes one of my hands and draws it away from my face. Electricity fizzes and jolts. It's too much—him touching me—and I almost tear my hand away.

"Easy," he murmurs. Holding it in his own, huge one, he rubs his thumb back and forth across my palm. I close my eyes, focus on breathing, and the jolts soften into tingles. His touch is doing me good. Underneath all the trembles, it's soothing.

"You lived in your pack, away from the human world, didn't you?"

I nod. Swallow hard. "Always. But I... I had to leave..." My voice is tight, constricted with the sobs that are threatening to break out. I fight to get it back under control. "I was in danger."

A low, rumbling growl rolls up from his chest. "What kind of danger?"

I clench my jaw. There's no way I can tell him what really happened. How a guy, not even one tenth as attractive as him rejected me publicly.

"My pack's feral," I say at last. "My mom smuggled me out because she thought I was going to be killed otherwise. *Or suffer a fate worse than death.* But it was dangerous for her, too—" I take a deep, calming breath. This I can tell him. "And as she was leaving me, she told me she's not even my mom."

He goes very still. Then his thick eyebrows draw together. "Did she explain how she wound up raising you?"

"Nope."

"I'm so sorry, girl."

When I dare drop my other hand from my face and look at him, the pain in his eyes seems to mirror my own.

"I'm not surprised you tried to turn yourself into a river rat," he says.

I gulp out a laugh, and suddenly, we're both laughing easily. Two pairs of eyes fixed on each other's, like there's an energy force connecting us.

"You gonna tell me your name?" he says softly, when our laughter falls away. I freak out a little when I realize he's still holding my hand, but I don't want to make a big deal of it by pulling away. Besides, it feels too nice. I can't help imagining how those rough hands of his would feel caressing me all over. Heat sweeps through me, leaving yearning in its wake.

"I don't really have a last name," I say. Only my pack name, which didn't officially belong to me, since I was a halfling. "My first name is Vanessa. I always hated it though."

He shrugs. "So, change it." He looks right into my eyes. His gaze is direct and pure. My river god who dragged me out of the depths.

Reborn.

The word shudders on the air.

"My mom called me Vani—" I break off, remembering my childhood fantasies, when I used to dream of having a different life entirely. "Savannah," I say. "I always wanted to be called Savannah."

"I like it. A woman's name." He nods approvingly.

Woman. A thrill goes through me. I've never thought of myself as a woman before. Not even when I was about to be mated and bred. Is that how this big, sexy man sees me?

"Suits you," he adds.

Not a halfling, or a river rat, but a *woman*. My skin tingles all over and I tear my eyes away, no longer brave enough to look at him.

"We'll get you some clothes that fit you properly. Some nicer stuff." His voice is low, lulling. I lean into it, drifting on fantasy.

"Some of those feminine toiletries."

Then I snap back to reality. My mom stuffed ten bucks into the pocket of my backpack. Aside from that, I have no money, at all. And why is this stranger being so kind to me? Mom warned me that guys who don't claim you as their mate are only after *one thing*.

I didn't really know what she meant, but now I do. And the thought of doing that thing with Beau is more exciting than I can say. But…I'm so confused.

I shoot a panicked glance at his home, which looks so nice and fancy. What does he want with me?

"It's a schoolie," he says.

"A-a what?"

"Used to be a school bus." He narrows his eyes questioningly. "They collect little kids, take them to school."

"I knew that," I say, and we smile at each other, because we both know I didn't.

He leans back in his chair. "Then you'll know they're generally bright yellow. But sometimes, when the municipality is done with them, you can buy em' up and convert them to your own luxury home."

"You converted this yourself?" I take in the pretty white and powder-blue exterior.

"Yup. Every last bit. It was a hobby of mine for a good six months. Now it's my full-time home. I've got a motorcycle, too. Sometimes, I take off on the bike. Other times, I hook the bike up with a trailer, and off we go to a new place."

"You always have your home with you," I murmur, thinking how incredible that would be.

"Pretty much." He looks happy at the thought.

"Can you show me around?" I blurt out.

He stills, and for a long time, he's silent, like he's fighting some internal battle.

I'm starting to regret asking, when he drags back his chair and leaps up. "Sure can."

As I stand up to join him, I'm struck again by how he towers over me. Such a big, powerfully-built guy, but he treats me with such gentleness.

He gestures to the bus. "Savannah, meet Bertha."

"You named your RV?" My heart gives a little flip.

His thick dark eyebrows tug together. "Of course. Would've been rude not to give this lady a name after all the time we've spent together."

A flutter of emotion goes through me. Something like jealousy. Something like a wish that he'd want to spend a lot of time with me. My cheeks heat again at my own silliness.

He holds the front door open for me and I go ahead of him, up the steps.

There's a lot of space in these schoolies. He shows me around, explaining how every bit of it was converted from a public bus into a home, and I explore it all, fascinated. I love the thought that he made all this with those big, strong hands of his. He shows me the kitchen, the seating area, the bathroom.

The only thing missing is a bed.

"Where do you sleep?" I ask.

"Up there." He points at what looks like a shelf, but he doesn't move to unfurl it from its recess, like all the other things he's shown me so far.

Together in this small space, his scent fills my nostrils. He smells like pine forests and leather and tobacco. I take several slow breaths in and out, each one flooding my body with euphoria. He's less than a foot away. If I take a step closer, we'll be touching. I can feel the heat of his body, and in the quiet I think I can hear his big heart thudding in time with mine. A beat of need. Of synchronicity.

His hands lift toward me, and I go real still, longing to feel them wrapping around my hips, pulling me against him.

His presence envelops me. My eyelids feel heavy and I let them flutter closed. My lips tingle.

There's a whoosh of movement in the air and my eyes snap open again.

He's stepped away.

"That's all," he says, in a businesslike voice.

I swallow down a boulder of disappointment. "T-thanks," I manage to choke out, embarrassment already smashing through desire. I imagine how I looked to him, eyes heavy, lips pursed.

Probably shameful.

He walks out of the bus, and I stumble after him.

THE SUN IS up in the sky now and it's turning out to be a bright, warm day. Beau strides off across the parking lot, and the tension between us severs. I wonder what I did wrong.

I go to the table and gather up the breakfast things, then I take them into the little kitchen and wash them up. When I come back out, he's pacing around a patch of pavement in a tight circle.

"Been thinking," he tells me, hands stuffed into the pockets of his shorts. "We need to get you someplace to stay."

"Yeah," I say, because he's right. "But—" *I barely have a cent to my name.*

"There's a bar over on the other side of town. Looks like they hire young people. Might have a room you can stay in."

"Great," I say with a brightness I don't feel. Which makes me a brat. Because twenty-four hours ago, that would've sounded like heaven. But now… now the last thing I want is to leave Beau's company.

Even though he's acting like he's desperate to see the back of me.

He looks at me assessingly. Then he darts indoors and returns with a small tool that he flicks open with an expert maneuver. A hunting knife. Before I know what's happening, he's grabbed the hem of the shirt I'm wearing and he's slicing off the last eight inches.

"No—!" I yelp. "What are you doing?"

"Almost done," he mutters, teeth gritted in concentration, and a moment later the excess fabric comes away.

"Your lovely shirt!" I examine the tattered ends.

"Need to make sure you look the part."

As I stand still, too stunned to move, he unfastens the last three buttons and ties the two loose ends together. The fabric pulls tight across my breasts and waist. I feel him drawing me closer, into him, as if he's molding me. A master craftsman, cinching me in his hands.

He stands back, measuring his handiwork. "Pretty," he says. Then he lifts a hand and sweeps my bangs to the side. They've gotten too long to hang straight down, and somehow he knows this. This raw, masculine man has a tenderness about him that I've never come across in a person before.

As his hand drops, his fingertip grazes my cheek, then the corner of my lips. So lightly, I wonder if I imagined it.

But that thought is enough; heat floods me, spreading down through my chest, to that spot between my thighs that hasn't quit aching since Beau came into my life.

"Too pretty. They're gonna love you." He says it in a strange way. Sad, almost angry, as if he doesn't like the thought of that. Then he turns away sharply.

"Been working on your shoes." He hands them to me. They're cheap, black canvas. Embarrassing, like the rest of my clothes. But they're no longer covered in river mud, and by some miracle, they're almost dry.

"Thank you, so much—" I mutter. Words are nothing like adequate to acknowledge what he's done for me.

"Can't have those little feet of yours wet all day." He coughs, casts around. "Are you about ready?"

I snatch up my dirty backpack, guilt flooding me. He probably had his whole day planned out before a little river rat intruded on it.

"Sure am." I force brightness into my voice.

He pulls on a pair of sneakers. "Let's go."

I follow him across the parking lot, confused as hell. A big hollow opening up inside me again.

3

Beau

$\mathcal{H}$eart crashing like a wrecking ball, I lead the little she-wolf across the crumbling parking lot. I stay two steps ahead of her, because if she was at my side, if I was able to see her at all right now, there's no way I'd be able to do this.

But I prick up my ears, listen for every step of those delicate feet as she keeps pace behind me.

Every bone, every nerve in my body is singing.

Take her back *home. She's yours.* My wolf's big dumb heart pulses beneath my ribcage like a drumbeat. Its fur burns my skin and my jaws ache for release. It wants out, demands to take possession of me.

But the threat of darkness prickles and sickens me. I can't go back to that place of rejection and madness.

Savannah is not mine.

There is no *mine* for a wolf like me.

I've been down that road before.

I had a pack once. An intended mate. She was in the pack next door—our friendly neighbors.

We grew up together, Kellie and I. In and out of each other's homes. We were each other's first everything: first slow dance, first kiss. Both of our packs expected us to end up together. To cement the bond between the two families. I would become Alpha of my pack and she would be queen.

As I was growing up, I was bursting with impatience. All I could think of was that day when we'd come of age and I'd make her mine. Give her my mark, and move into the roles that were waiting for us. I never even entertained the thought that there could be anyone else for either of us.

Then she chose another.

A wolf from a hostile pack, a lifelong enemy of mine.

I couldn't blame her. Her wolf had made the choice, driven by the fates that had been mysteriously silent all of our short lives.

But it tore me apart. It was an agony I'd lacked the imagination to anticipate. I blamed my pack—all those people who'd spoken so confidently of our union, and had never hinted to my dumb, naïve self that it might not be in my stars.

I went feral. I fought almost everyone; scared the hell out of everyone else, and just about destroyed my own pack in my rage and grief.

Then my wolf burst out of me and refused to go

back in. After it attacked Kellie's new mate in a bloody battle, there was no going back.

I had to leave.

I lost two years trapped in my wolf form. I used the last of my strength to force the beast into a vast wilderness and keep it there, and it ran wild among the trees, savage and desperate.

Little by little, I began to gain some control over it. To feel my human self rising to the surface again. Until one day, I caught it off-guard, exhausted and half-asleep, and I ripped out of it, and became a man again.

I shaped up. I snuck back to my pack and took some inheritance I was owed, and I went about setting myself up in the human world. My one requirement: I couldn't stay in one place for long. I needed to be on the road, to keep my wolf active and distracted, so it wouldn't go getting any ideas about hunting down a mate again.

I learned that humans value shifters for their superior senses and strength, and I carved out a career as a bounty hunter-slash-investigator.

And so, I've lived like this for these years. A lone wolf with alpha blood running in my veins, in my little motorhome, with my bike and my trailer, keeping the madness away.

The one thing I know is, now I've gotten myself back, broken away from the madness, there's no way I'm going to give it up again.

Not even for purest soul, whose heart seems to beat in time with my own. Matched with the prettiest cherry lips and the curviest little body. Because it's a package sweet enough to drive my wolf to destruction again.

Once you've stared into the abyss, there's no way you'll return to it by choice.

WHEN WE REACH THE CROSSWALK, I wait for Savannah to catch up. It's rush hour—which doesn't mean a lot in this little town, but my protective instinct has gone into overdrive. This is one last thing I can do for her.

She stops at my side and looks at me expectantly. It's adorable the way she tilts her chin up to see me, because she's so much shorter than me.

But when she flicks her long bangs out of her eyes, those glass green irises catch the light and they annihilate me all over again.

I'm dead. If I don't get her out of my sight A-sap, my wolf will destroy me.

The pedestrian signal is showing red. "You know how to cross the street, right?" I say.

She rolls her eyes. "I haven't spent all my life in the stone age, you know. My pack often goes to human markets to sell our goods. Used to have my own stall, actually."

I can't resist a smile. She's got spirit. A fierce little flame in her chest that burns amid all her suffering.

I long to ask what kind of stall she had, but I don't.

No more learning about her. No more wondering, stoking my interest. This ends right here.

"The bar's just down here," I say, gesturing to an alleyway. I came across it a couple of days ago while I was roaming around the town. I'm not antisocial by nature; I do like company sometimes.

Truth is, I yearn to share my life with another—
I cut that thought right off.

That way madness lies.

When you travel a lot, you get an instinct for the kinds of places that might welcome a lone wolf—or be a safe haven for a little she-wolf.

From the outside, *Sinner's Refuge* looks kinda dilapidated—old red-brick walls, running to two stories. Battered old balcony rail on the upper level, a barred window and a dark-red front door at street level. Peeling paint, rust. Seen better days, but the kind of place that could feel like home—at least, I sure hope so.

I push open the front door and let Savannah through. She moves stiffly, and I see the tension in her shoulders, the bravery in the set of her jaw. I want to snatch her up in my arms, bring her right back to Bertha, and never let her go.

But I can't. Can't fall apart like that again.

Instead, I drag my eyes away from the flash of cleavage showing at the top of her—*my*—shirt. The full curve of her ass as she passes in front of me. Pretend my cock doesn't swell every time my gaze alights on her sweet body. She might be short, but she's all woman. Enough to get any werewolf's mouth watering…

And right on cue, my wolf breaks out a snarl, ready to defend her from any other suitors.

Inside, the bar is wood paneled, cozy red benches around the edges of the room, battered tables and chairs in the center.

It's still early and the only occupants are a skinny chick perched on a bar stool in the corner, and the bar owner, who's behind the bar, arms folded on the counter. Just like yesterday, she fixes me with a suspicious look, like she's considering throwing me out on my ass. Who was it who said they'd never join a club that would have them as a member?

Some smart ass, but I can't fault the sentiment.

Yesterday, I made the mistake of showing a photo around. I'm on the trail of a fugitive, but turns out doing that kind of thing around here is *verboten*. Very fucking *verboten*, and likely to get the shit kicked out of you. Not many people could kick my ass, but I wouldn't put it past this tough old bear shifter to try.

She straightens herself up to her full height, which is good six inches shorter than me, frizzy brown hair sticking out around her head. Her eyes blaze with sternness. "Thought I told you—" she begins.

I raise my hands. "Not staying. Just brought someone with me." I lay a hand on Savannah's back. The warmth of her skin floods to my fingertips and I pull away sharply. *Sheesh*, this is some unearthly damned attraction. The sooner I get away, the better.

"This is Savannah. She's new in town and she's looking for work. Maybe a bed and board kind of arrangement. She's real reliable. Strong. Hard-working." I'm just guessing at these parts, but I get the sense Savannah is all those things and more.

When the bear shifter turns her golden eyes on Savannah, they stop blazing so hard, and she looks almost kind.

"You got any experience at bar work, hun?"

Savannah nods eagerly. "I'm a quick learner, too."

The woman taps a finger against her lips, looks thoughtful. "Don't think I've got any spare beds right now. We're all full up."

"Oh, I can sleep on the floor, anything," Savannah says fast.

She shrugs. "If you don't mind roughing it, I guess there's plenty of floor space."

Savannah gives a little gasp. "That mean I've got the job?"

She throws her arms wide. "Welcome to the team, hun. Can you start now?"

"Just a minute—" I butt in. "Where is this floor space?"

The woman blinks. "Upstairs."

"Who are the other people in there?"

"There's a girls' dorm and a guys' dorm."

"But is it secure?"

"Yup. The door locks. Everyone has their own key."

"Can I take a look?"

She rolls her eyes, but then she beckons me through the bar, and out the back to a set of stairs.

"Come, too," I tell Savannah. "Check you'll be happy here."

She scuttles after me with a shy smile, her cheeks pink. "Thank you," she whispers to me.

"Just need to make sure you're safe," I say gruffly, belying the rush of happiness that flooded my chest.

The bar owner shows us to a neat, eight-bed dorm, with an en suite bathroom, and a secure lock on the door. There's a space by the window where Savannah can sleep. The bar owner says she might be able to dig out an air mattress or something.

"Okay?" She raises her eyebrows, like I'm the fussiest guy in the world.

I don't care. Making sure Savannah has a safe place to stay is all I care about.

"Guess so," I say. I don't love the thought of Savannah staying there, but seems about the best option right now.

We all go back downstairs. And my heart plummets like the devil's drop from heaven. Because Savannah doesn't need me anymore. I've got no reason to hang around.

"Take care of her," I tell the woman.

She rolls her eyes again, but I sense I can trust her. There's a good heart under that cranky exterior.

"So long," I say to Savannah and I give a casual wave, ignoring the urge to throw my arms around her.

She turns, her sweet face full of questions.

"I'm leaving town now." I jerk my thumb over my shoulder. *Dang.* Don't normally get awkward like that. "All the best for the future."

She goes pale and her face crumples for the second time today. "You're leaving? You didn't tell me."

"I'm always on the move, darlin'. Gotta earn my keep. Keep Bertha in gas."

Her pink cherry lips work. "But—?" comes out in a choked gasp.

"Maybe we'll cross paths again," I bark out. Then I turn on my heel, so I don't have to look at her again.

The door slams behind me and I'm back outside.

When I inhale, my breath comes in all ragged and broken. I start walking fast. The danger's passed and I'm free.

But it doesn't feel like that at all.

It feels like I've lost something I'll miss forever.

4

Savannah

I stare at the spot where Beau disappeared,
long after he's gone.

He was sure glad to be rid of me. I didn't even get to
thank him for all he's done. The truth is, when he
turned his back on me, a stab of loss robbed me of all
my words.

It's crazy. I've only known him for a few hours, but I
have the weirdest feeling we've always known each
other.

And now he's gone.

I'm bursting to rush after him, beg him not to go.
Get his contact details at the very least.

But I guess if he'd wanted me to have them, he
would've given them to me.

I squirm as that moment in the RV hurtles back to

me again. That dumb moment when I thought he *liked me* liked me. Thought he was going to kiss me.

But then he saw something he didn't like at all and he pulled away.

It's okay, I'm used to it.

Just wish it didn't hurt even more than being rejected in public while buck naked.

"Come behind the bar, hun." My new employer's voice is softer now. She holds up the bar flap and lets me slip through.

"I'm Meredith. That little stick insect down the end of the bar is Elinor."

The girl who's been folded up on a bar stool looks up from her phone and salutes goofily.

Meredith shows me around—the glasses racks, the glass washer. The fridges, beer taps. House liquors, top shelf. I nod knowledgably. I wasn't lying when I told her I had experience—I've worked my pack's makeshift bar a ton. But this feels like a comfortable, friendly place.

Meredith holds a battered glass up to the light and examines it, frowning. "First rule of working at Sinner's Refuge: don't ask the customers any leading questions."

"Leading?" I say.

She gives me a hard look. "Anything that puts a person the spot. Makes them uncomfortable. Not want to drink here."

"Okay. I can do that."

"In return, folks won't ask you anything that'll make you feel uncomfortable. Lotsa wanted posters here. Folks turning up looking for their people. Not everyone wants to be found. Can cause a lot of trouble. Cops sniffing around and all."

"No one's looking for me," I say quickly.

"Good," she replies, but I hardly hear her, because another wave of grief is knocking me sideways.

For a few beautiful hours, Beau made me forget my pack. Showed me I could live again. But now that he's gone, that loss—of everything I knew—opens up like a crater.

"Best keep busy." Meredith is looking at me kindly. She squeezes my arm. "Whenever you're ready, we're listening, hun. Looks like you've been through a lot."

I nod, because if I say anything at all right now, I might burst into tears.

It's quiet for a couple of hours, then it gets busy at lunchtime. Meredith's sister turns up—a statuesque, gray-haired lady—and she and Meredith get to work in the kitchen, while Elinor and I work the bar. Elinor is a whirl-wind, darting from table to table, taking orders at a hectic pace, sneaking up behind me to crack jokes and observa-tions about the customers. She's some kind of shifter but I don't know what. Her animal scent is weak, like mine, maybe. She's very skinny, with protruding, wide-set eyes, and a small mouth. She has a bunch of piercings, and her hair is long and glossy black. She reminds me of some kind of bird. A raven or a magpie. I don't know anything about other species. Maybe it's not polite to ask.

After the lunchtime rush is over, it gets real quiet

again, and Meredith emerges from the kitchen with a huge leather purse slung over her shoulder.

"I'm heading out for a while," she says. "Think you girls can hold the fort?"

"Well, I don't know." Elinor bites her lip and her googly eyes shoot around the almost-deserted room.

"Don't get smart, Elinor," Meredith says wearily. "I want you to set a good example for my newest employee."

"Course, boss." Elinor offers her goofy salute again and Meredith stomps out, sighing.

"She likes to act like a ball-breaker, but she has a real warm heart underneath," Elinor says as soon as the front door has slammed shut.

"Compared to my pack, she's an angel," I say.

Elinor pauses in her task of polishing wine glasses. "You had a pack?"

"Yup." I yank open the dishwasher and pull out a rack of steaming glasses, needing to keep my hands busy. "I was, but I kind of got rejected, by my intended. Then, things got weird."

She bites her lip and tilts her head to look at me sideways.

Definitely a bird shifter.

"That's so rough," she says. "I never had my own flock. I got rejected when I was still a baby. Kicked out of the nest…figuratively speaking," she adds, when I look shocked.

"Got raised by some humans for a while, but it didn't work out," she continues. "And I worked my way over here. Heard this was a place where people didn't mock you for your differences."

"It's cool you found it," I say. I start to ask her something else, then I break off. It's kind of tricky not being able to ask all the questions that are bouncing around in my head.

"You can ask standard questions," she says, as if she's read my mind. "But nothing too, personal, you know."

"Like?" I ask.

"Like—" She casts her eyes up to the ceiling. "Like I should definitely not ask you who that guy was who brought you here."

"That. guy—" I murmur. And the force of Beau's presence hits me like a bullet train.

How to explain what Beau was to me? A river god, who found me under the bridge and dragged me out of the mud. Breathed life back into me. Lit me up inside for the very first time in my life.

"He's sweet on you," Elinor interrupts my thoughts.

Heat floods me, and I can tell I'm blushing all the way to the roots of my hair. *Crap.* I hate it when that happens. "No, he's not," I say firmly. *Quite the opposite, in fact. He couldn't wait to get away from me.*

"He couldn't take his eyes off you."

My breath catches in my chest.

But that couldn't be true.

He wouldn't have left if it was.

"Well, he's gone now. That's the last I'll see of him."

Elinor gives me a sly look, like a magpie that has caught up something shiny in its beak. "Don't count on it."

"You live here, too?" I ask, eager to change the subject.

"Yeah, along with… seven other girls." She counts on her fingers. "Meredith looks after us. She doesn't have any cubs of her own, and we're like her kids. A bunch of rejects. I call us the Jects." She does a silly dance. "The Jects of Perdue Town. P-Town!" she finishes triumphantly.

I wrinkle my nose.

She throws her hands up. "P-Town…like Chi-Town, ya know?"

"Nah, doesn't have the same ring to it." I grin, shake my head at her dorkiness. It's just what I need to take my mind off Beau.

The door clangs open and a couple of guys amble in. They're both big all over, but especially in the shoulders. Pale blond hair, light blue eyes. They could be brothers. Some type of bear shifters, I think.

Elinor makes a cawing sound of dismay. "Crap, those two are assholes," she mutters. "Meredith usually gets rid of them."

"Ladies." Both guys clump to the bar, plonk their elbows and upper bodies down on the counter and survey the beer taps.

The taller one leers at Elinor. "What's up, Skinny Minnie?"

"I told you not to call me that," she snaps.

He gives her a slow smile, full of insolence. "And who's your sexy friend?"

I'm touched when Elinor steps in front of me. She's no match for two bears, but I admire her fierceness.

"She's not here to be spoken to like that." She plants her hands on her bony hips. "Now, either you order a drink or you get the hell out of here!"

The other one sucks his teeth. "No need to be so snippy, Skinny Minnie."

I pray for them to leave. Something weird is going on inside me. Their presence is making me all riled up and shaky, and my skin won't quit burning.

But they order a couple of beers. And when they've paid, they don't take a table, but continue to hang over the bar.

"It's seating in here, only," Elinor says. She's chopping up limes so fast her knife is a blur.

"Is that right?" The taller of the two guys continues to gawk at me.

I want to untie my shirt, so it hangs loose on me, but I can't bring myself to undo Beau's handiwork.

"Tell me your name, hot stuff."

"Not relevant," I snap.

He slides his meaty hands across the bar top so they're dangling over my side. "Oh, *nothing* could be more relevant right now, baby. Aren't you a juicy little treat?"

There's strange growling sound at the back of my throat, which I swear I didn't make myself.

Unfortunately, meathead number one pricks up his ears. "Oh, *Feisty.* Love a bit of a fight in a chick." He snaps his teeth together.

Elinor slinks up behind me. "Meredith should be back any time now," she mutters.

Then her voice turns ear-splitting as she yells, "You need to leave, right now!"

"Fuck!" Meathead number one jams his fingers in his ears. "You could deafen a person, you know that?" He raises his beer glass and chugs the whole thing down. "I'll leave when I'm done, birdbrain." He slams the empty glass down on the counter. "Gimme another."

"You're barred. Get the hell out of here!" Elinor jabs a skinny arm toward the door. I glance at this tiny, brave girl in admiration. This beast could snap her with his little finger, but she's not backing down.

"Or what?" His eyes are small and mean, whites turned pink. He's already drunk; I smell the alcohol coming off him in waves.

Instinctively, I gather Elinor up behind me, and I back away, toward the door that leads to the kitchen.

He lifts his head and sniffs hard, and a look of delight crosses his face. "Aw, don't run away, little wolf. You know how much a big old bear loves a chase."

He steps back, gathers himself, and *leaps*. His huge bulk crash-lands on top of the bar. He lands clumsily, hunched up on all fours, scattering glasses and napkins in all directions.

Another low growl bursts from my throat, and my skin burns. It feels like all my hairs are standing on end, and they're prickly, as if they're made from tiny quills. Something is happening inside me. Something that's scaring the hell out of me. I gasp for breath as my insides start to crunch and twist excruciatingly.

"Come here, little wolf. Come to daddy," he croons.

I back away some more, wondering what the hell I'll do if he grabs me now.

The front door bursts open.

And I stop breathing altogether.

Because there is Beau.

His big sexy frame fills the doorway. Shoulders massive, hands hanging loose at his sides. Blue eyes narrow and blazing as he takes in the scene.

He didn't leave.

My heart shudders in my chest.

My knees tremble.

Every little bit of me longs to run to him, throw myself into his arms.

He strides across the bar, his feet pounding on the floorboards. And his voice booms, like the voice of a god, capable of knocking mortal beings senseless:

"You've got two seconds to get the hell out of here, before I turn you and your brother into a pair of fluffy white rugs."

The big oaf shuffles around on the bar until he can see who's addressing him.

He's beefier than Beau, but he lacks his pure muscle, and as his eyes turn shifty, I can see he knows it. Totally outclassed.

Beau doesn't give him any more time to think. He strides over, grabs him by the back of his shirt, and hauls him right off the bar. Then, keeping ahold of him, he drags him to the other side of the room, where his brother is standing paralyzed. Beau snatches his brother up, too, and aims the two of them at the door, one after the other, like a pair of bowling balls.

They tumble through, with two almighty crashes.

I hold my breath, expecting them to return, but they're gone. There's a flash of color as their bulky shapes pass the barred windows.

Then I turn back to Beau.

He's standing in the middle of the room, feet apart, all relaxed like the past couple of minutes didn't just happen. He's an alpha. His power pours off him in waves. I feel it, deep in my bones.

Then his eyes lock onto mine, and he's there, at the bar, his big hands reaching for me. "Are you okay, girl?"

I take two quick strides and lay my own hands in his. They're warm, and they wrap around mine, wrap around my soul. His touch feels like home.

I close my eyes, relief flooding through me. "I thought you were leaving."

He doesn't reply right away, and when I open my eyes again, the vulnerability in his handsome face startles me.

"I couldn't," he says shortly.

My lips purse into a *why*, but I can't bring myself to form the word.

"I needed to protect you."

Protect me.

I draw a deep breath and it comes out ragged. "H-how did you know what was happening?"

"I didn't." His cornflower blue eyes are steady.

Trembles go through me, and I start to shake all over. Because I think I grasp his meaning. He leans closer, his lips swim toward mine. My heart hammers and yearning, anticipation rises up in me. I edge closer, closer—

And the front door bursts open again.

"You again? Thought you were leaving." Meredith's voice blasts across the room.

We jerk apart.

"And a good evening to you, too." Beau turns unhurriedly and throws her a casual smile. And my heart flips. Because he's absolutely gorgeous.

She storms over, takes in the shattered glass and spilled tableware. "You been causing trouble?"

"He saved us from two nasty men," Elinor pipes up from the other side of the bar. I'd forgotten about her. And my cheeks warm at the thought of what she just saw happen between Beau and me.

She stalks over, hands on her hips. "We would've been toast if he hadn't arrived when he did."

"I'm not sure that's true," Beau drawls. "Think these girls were doing a pretty good job of holding their own."

My skin prickles as I realize he's looking at me with something like admiration.

"Oh, it's totally true. We would've been eaten alive," Elinor shrills, flapping her hands. She's hectic, upset by all the disturbance.

"Well, good job, all of you." Meredith scans the three of us, a ghost of a smile tugging at her lips.

"Guess I owe you a free meal," she says to Beau.

"Oh, I'm not hungry yet—" His eyes flicker to me. "I'll accept a beer though."

"Sure thing." Meredith barges behind the bar and pulls it herself, before placing it in front of him with a flourish. "You're free to drink here from now on. Long as you don't cause any trouble."

Beau raises his glass. "No trouble, guaranteed. You won't even know I'm here."

He slinks off to a corner and settles down on a high stool with a contented sigh.

It gets busy again and I try to focus on my work, but all I can think about is the big wolf shifter lolling at the end of the bar, sipping his beer, scanning his phone and, very often, turning his burning eyes on me.

Whenever we happen look at each other at the same moment, a fork of lightning sizzles through me, rocking my body from head to toe. How am I supposed to focus and chat to customers, when I can hardly breathe? When Beau scorches my skin with his gaze?

Just before seven p.m., another girl turns up to take over my shift, and Meredith tells me I'm done for the day.

"Good job," she says and hands me a bunch of bills.

Cash. Money of my own. I want to hug her.

Beau dumps his empty glass on the counter. "You ready?" he says.

I blink. "For what?"

"To go home, of course."

"But I'm staying here."

He shakes his head calmly. "No, you're not. You're coming with me."

"I am?"

"Of course." He says it like it's the most obvious thing in the world, and my heart soars.

Because I want to go home with him, back to Bertha, more than I've wanted anything in my life.

Beau picks up my backpack, raises a hand to Meredith and Elinor, and saunters outside.

For a few seconds I freeze, caught in indecision. Worrying that he didn't *really* mean it.

Then I hurry after him, heart pounding like a jackhammer.

But when I hit the sidewalk, I turn circles in confusion.

He's nowhere to be seen.

5

Beau

My wolf howls and frets. Burning my skin, tearing me up inside.

Fuck, it's too much for me to control. I slip into a nearby alleyway, force it back down, deep inside me.

It's been hell today. The worst it's been ever since I lost control of it years back.

How could you leave her? it's been bellowing from my guts, like it has a life of its own.

I tried my damned hardest.

After I tore myself away from Savannah's sweet presence, I knew I had to get out of town if I was going to stand a chance of survival.

I went back to my RV, hooked up my trailer, hauled my bike on. I even started Bertha up and drove a little.

Then I pulled over on the highway and I sat, staring

at the road ahead. My heart pumping hard enough to knock me out.

Every last bit of me was screaming to turn around, go back to Perdue Town.

She's mine.

My mate.

Take her.

Protect her.

Lightning doesn't strike twice.

Except for that one part of me—the part that had dragged my human self out of my wolf when I was lost in the forest, kept me sane all these years. Turned my head away from pretty girls who flirted with me.

Kept me alone and healthy and level-headed.

Was I really gonna throw all of that away?

Risk going back to that dark, dark place, of madness and inhumanity?

Even the thought of it cracked open that deep, deep chasm. Bony fingers of darkness clutching at me, dragging me down.

Well, I started up Bertha again, drove some more.

But I didn't get very far before my hands froze. Could hardly get them to unclench enough to work the gear stick.

This went on a couple more times, and the whole time, my head was full of her.

My mate. The one my soul had craved all these years.

Because this thing I feel for Savannah, it's like nothing else.

How could a man walk away from something like this and continue to live?

The life he'd have would be no life at all.

"Beau?" comes the voice of a pure angel. It pours through me like honey, trickles into my soul.

Crap, she's out already. I thought she'd be another minute, fighting her own demons.

I step out from the alleyway just in time to catch her as she comes past.

She's a vision.

Those tight, black leggings clinging to her sexy round hips, and that old shirt I gave her resurrected, embracing her full, round tits. Long bangs hanging sexily over one eye, and the rest of her wavy, reddish black hair bouncing around her shoulders. Her cherry lips part in surprise as she sees me, her eyes widen, and that's all the encouragement I need.

I wrap my arms around her and draw her deep into the alleyway. I back her against the wall, she tilts her head up, and finally, our mouths meet in a union of angels and demons.

Christ, those lips are soft, pillowy, and they open under mine with a shiver. I slide my tongue in and when I find the tip of hers, I almost levitate. She's all silk and velvet.

Soft, sweet moans escape her throat, and she clings to me like she needs me, like she's been needing me all day. And I don't hold back; I wrap her tight in my arms, feeling her sweet curves pressing into me. When I cup her ass in both hands, lifting, she bounces up, just like I hoped she would, and wraps her legs up, around my waist. She's so tiny in my arms, yet so womanly. No longer the broken waif I rescued from the riverbank, but a sexy woman who knows exactly what she wants.

When I draw away, she whispers, "Beau, don't stop," in that sexy voice of hers and I dive right back in, kissing her deeper, deeper.

My cock swells for the tenth time that day, pressing against her warm core. And the sweet scent of her arousal filters up like nectar.

She wants me like I want her. The realization shudders through me, and my wolf growls deep in my throat —its sound of barely suppressed need.

Her fingers dig into the back of my neck and her kisses get hungrier, more demanding, her tongue darting into my mouth, dancing around mine.

If we don't quit, we're going to make a spectacle of ourselves out here.

Reluctantly, I draw back and let her sweet body slide down to the ground. She staggers a little. Her eyes flame pure emerald fire and her cheeks are flushed. I see her nipples are erect, stiff peaks beneath the fabric of my shirt. My desire is like a red mist. The world could fall away right now and I would see nothing but her.

"Let's get home," I say gruffly. Too keyed up to say anything else.

"Yes." She nods quickly.

This time I don't walk ahead of her, but I reach for her hand. She laces her fingers into mine. And what a feeling it is, those soft, delicate fingers almost lost in my big paw.

I force myself to go slow, to walk at the pace of her

slender legs, although I yearn to pick her up and run with her.

There's no rush, I tell my wolf. If she's truly my mate, we have all the time in the world.

But every second feels like a torture.

At last, Bertha comes into view, on the far side of the cracked old parking lot. We were silent all the way, tension crackling like static between us. But now, she says, "we're home," in a breathy way, and those words wrap around my heart with hope.

When we get close, I sweep her up in my arms again and carry her up the steps and through the door.

I curse myself that the bed isn't set up. Instead, I bring her over to the couch. It's a comfy place to relax at least—I made sure of that when I installed it. The cushions are all soft and inviting.

I sit down and lean back so she's straddling my lap, my curvy goddess, arching above me.

Desire and uncertainty are at war in her eyes, turning her irises stormy.

Slowly, I raise my hands and cup her lovely round tits through the fabric of the shirt, chafe those hard nipples with my thumbs.

She gives a little cry. She's tightly wound. My cock surges, pressing at her core.

I unfasten the buttons on the shirt, like I've done a hundred times before—but now it's embracing the sexy body of my little she-wolf.

Her bra is sweet, simple, and I make short work of it, pulling it down so her lovely breasts spring out.

But I barely glimpse her rose-bud nipples, before her

hands fly up to cover them. I ease off, kiss her sweet cherry lips some more, until she relaxes.

"You don't need to be shy with me, honey," I growl into the side of her neck and she gives a little gasp.

It's a sensitive spot, I can tell. I make a trail of kisses all the way down her neck, adding little nibbles here and there, and she sighs at each one. I move to the gorgeous hollow between her collarbones, then lower, lower toward her cleavage. When I finally reach her tits, she drops her hands and bares them for me, eagerly guiding her right nipple into my mouth.

I lick the sweet bud, and when I suck on it a little, she moans, showing me just how much she likes it. She shuffles forward, riding up against my sternum, fingers tugging on my hair while she presses her nipple deeper into my mouth. Right, then left, then right again. They taste of cherries, just like her lips, and I could suck on them all night long. My cock rages, fit to burst, straining painfully against my zipper, and I long to unleash it, bury it deep inside her. She's ready for me; my nose is full of her arousal, her pussy hot and damp against my chest. I shuffle her back a little, slide my hand down the front of her leggings, into her panties.

"Fuck, Beau," she chokes out.

Christ, she's wetter than I thought possible. A cascade of yearning. And so soft. When I curve my hand around her pussy, she rides against it. Grinds her clit against my palm. I try to slip a finger inside her. She's so tight, so small. No man has been here before. My cock pulses at the thought. I'm close; too close. I finger her lightly, not wanting to hurt her, and I feel her little pussy clenching around my finger. When I hold still, she moves her hips up and down, riding me. Hungry for the pleasure I can give her. Her scent is driving me wild.

"I need to taste you," I whisper in her ear.

I hear her breath catch.

"Taste me?" she says, like she's never heard of such a thing before, and I fall for her a little bit more.

"Lick you all over," I say. And I flip her off my lap, lay her on her back and resume my mission of worshipping every last bit of her.

Cupping her full tits in my hands, I kiss her all over her lovely soft belly. Then I hook my fingers into the waistband of her leggings and ease them down little by little, planting kisses all the way.

When a thatch of dark red pubic hair emerges, I damn near come in my pants. It's all I can do not to hump her leg. Keeping her distracted with my mouth, I slide her leggings and drenched panties right off. When I slide my tongue over the tiny bud of her clit, she falls open with a groan of need. I take a moment to take her in. My beautiful little she-wolf, all naked, spread out for me.

"Beautiful," I tell her, so beautiful. And I lick her little pussy, scented like nectar and heaven. I go back and forth, licking, sucking on her tiny bud, figuring out what she likes, and before long she starts tugging on my hair, her hips jerking up and down.

"Yes, come for me, darlin'," I mutter.

"I-I've never—" she gasps, and a shiver of delight goes through me.

"Come for the first time with me. I want to taste your first orgasm on my tongue."

"Oh, god," she moans. She shudders and shudders, and with a sharp cry she climaxes, right before my eyes.

It's incredible. The most goddamn incredible thing I've ever experienced in my life. All honey and sweetness and soft velvety thighs.

"You made me... made me..." she murmurs, minutes later.

"Come?" I supply.

"Yeah, that," she laughs. "I didn't know..."

She's casting around for the unfamiliar words, and my heart blooms with tenderness. So innocent, but so ready for pleasure. All this passion bottled up inside her. It's a wondrous thing to see.

"Did you like it?" I ask teasingly.

"Like it?" She puffs out a breath of air. "That's an understatement. I thought I was going to explode or something. Is that normal?"

"Yup, sounds pretty standard," I say, while warmth floods my veins. I gather her up in my arms and pepper her face with kisses.

When I lay her back on the couch again, she reaches for my cock. I let out a hiss between gritted teeth. It's so hard for her, it hurts. The mating urge pounds through my body like a drumbeat.

I go very still, hardly daring to breathe as her soft, exploratory hand pulls down my zipper, reaches in and draws out my cock. When she grasps it for the first time, it surges, and I bite back a growl.

Claim her.

Mark her.

My wolf is close to the surface. My body is alight with need for her.

She wants this, my little princess, her eyelids heavy with desire as she slides her hand up and down my girth, catching up my pre-cum and lubricating her hand with it as she milks me.

But if I mate her now, there's no going back for either of us.

All these years, I've waited, waited. Never once giving in to the mating urge.

Holding back. Staying sane.

She leans closer, her tender mouth latching onto mine, as her hand moves up and down.

I force back my primal urge, and I let my climax come.

I let go; explode, shooting a jet of cum all over her breasts and belly.

"I'm sorry!" she yelps as my climax pulses out of me, my seed spent on her lovely skin.

I flop back against the couch cushions with a groan. "What for?"

"I screwed up, didn't I?"

"Not at all. That was… that was wonderful."

She bites her lip and gives a nervous laugh. "I guess I got scared. I mean, I wanted to, but…"

Tenderness washes over me, as I pull her into my arms. "You didn't do anything wrong at all." I press a kiss to her temple and keep my mouth there, inhaling her heavenly scent. "There's nothing to be scared of," I murmur.

But her eyes are bright with anxiety, and it worries me. "What is it, Savannah?"

She pulls away from me, her features taut. "Will it hurt a lot when we mate?"

I frown. "Maybe a little the first time. But then it'll feel real good."

Her nostrils flare and I hear her breathing, fast and shallow. "In my pack…I used to hear awful sounds when the alphas were mating their females."

A stab of pain lances my heart. I stroke her face gently. "No, it won't be like that at all, I promise. It'll be like the climax you just had, but a whole lot better."

She looks so dubious, it kills me.

"Here's what we're going to do. We'll get dressed, cook some dinner, relax a little, and then you're going to tell me about your pack, okay? And I'm not going to hurt you, ever." I lift her hand and press it to my lips. "You hear me?"

Finally, she breaks into a smile.

I gather up the shards of my heart and make a vow— that nothing will hurt this girl ever again. I'll protect her with everything I've got.

Even if it costs me my sanity.

6

Savannah

can hardly look at Beau as we get dressed. I can't believe I just made such a fool of myself. He'd already made me feel so amazing, and I wanted him so bad, I was aching for him.

And then I screwed up.

I just couldn't stand the thought that this thing between us that felt so beautiful could turn into that ugly roaring and screaming I used to hear at the territory. When I was a kid, it used to wake me up at night. I'd jam a pillow against my ears, trying to block it out. I didn't know what it was, just that it was connected to the reason why the women always looked so miserable in their harems.

But Beau said he'd never hurt me, and I think I

believe him. This man who's strong enough to throw two bears out on their asses is so gentle with me.

But what if…what if things are different after we mate? What if some guys are kind until they possess you?

My mom's parting words burn my ears again:

Don't give your heart away to a man.

Beau slips outside ahead of me. I think he wants to give me some privacy. And I'm grateful for it. I take my time freshening up, brushing my hair which has gotten very mussed. Not a whole lot I can do about my drenched panties right now.

I TAKE out a plastic bag from my backpack, full of the wet clothes I was wearing yesterday. I figure I'll go wash them in the river, see if Beau has a drying rack I can use.

I wonder what he's thinking about me now. He was treating me like I was a woman, but now he's probably thinking I'm just a silly little girl. He proudly hooks up with girls every time he stops in a new town, brings them back to his bus. Drives them wild.

Bile rises up in my throat. I can't stand the thought of him being with other women. It's dumb. He's a decade older than me. Of course he's been with a ton of women. And of course he's not the settling down kind, he's made that clear. He must have had women falling at his feet all his life. Guess he's a guy who doesn't want to have a mate.

Just as well I didn't let him fuck me, I think, as I step outside the van.

Beau has pulled a grill out of somewhere, and the coals are already glowing hot.

"Getting her cranked up for dinner." He throws me a lazy grin when I emerge, like there's not a single tense thought in his mind.

I wave the plastic bag awkwardly. "Going to go wash some clothes."

He frowns. "In the river?"

"Yup. I've washed clothes in the river all my life," I mutter. Now I feel even more ashamed.

"Okay." He shrugs carelessly.

I HEAD over to the riverbank. It's near twilight, and the water is dark now. So different from the shimmering gold of the morning.

Did all of this happen in a single day? It's so weird. I feel like Beau and I have known each other for a long time. For forever, really. But less than twenty-four hours ago, I couldn't even have imagined meeting someone like him.

I scramble down the side of the bank and dunk my clothes in the flow of the water. The mud is sticky, like it was on my skin. I hold the clothes up, examine them critically in the fading light. Maybe when I've done a few shifts at the bar, I'll be able to go shopping, buy some less embarrassing stuff.

When I get back, Beau is hard at work at the grill. A bunch of meat is cooking and it smells all kinds of awesome. Guilt flows through me as I remember this is the second time he's cooked for me today. "Let me take over," I say.

"This?" He points his cooking tongs at the grill. "Nope. Barbecuing is guys' work. I put out a clothes rack for you, on the other side of Bertha." He tilts his head in the general direction. "And if you want something to do, go grab us a couple of beers from the fridge."

I lay out my clothes, select two beers from a small but tidy fridge, dig out a couple of plates and some silverware, and bring everything outside.

It's dark by the time dinner is ready. Beau turns on a light at the edge of the awning, and it casts a soft glow over the surroundings.

"One more thing." He darts inside and returns with a candle in a jar, which he positions in the middle of the table.

"Like it?" The glance he throws me is tinged with uncertainty. "Only, I don't normally have company."

"It's…it's perfect," I say, thinking it's the most romantic thing I've seen in my life. My silly heart flutters as I sit down opposite him.

The beer is ice cold and the grilled meat is delicious. "Hunted it myself," Beau tells me.

THE FIRST FEW sips of beer relax me, smooth over my sharp edges.

Beau asks me about the bar, and I tell him about Elinor. How she calls us The Jects.

"She sounds like fun," he says.

"She is," I agree. "She said this is a famous reject town. Guess that's why my mom brought me here."

Beau is looking at me with amusement. "Home for losers, misfits, and ne'er do wells."

"Is that true?"

He shrugs. "I don't know. I was just passing through for work."

"You were looking for someone?"

"I received intelligence he might have blown through here." He stretches his feet out in front of him, gazes at the darkening sky.

I study him while his attention is directed away from me. "I really screwed up your day, didn't I?"

He jerks forward and lays his big hand on mine, his gaze intense. "No, honey. Not at all. Trust me, you were the best part of my day."

A prickly kind of heat sweeps through me. "But don't you need to find this guy?" I manage to say.

"Nope. If I don't find him, someone else will. It's no big deal."

I frown, wondering if that's true. Wondering what he gave up to help me.

I ask him all about his job. Sure sounds like fun tracking people down, hunting for obscure pieces of information. I can see it suits him well, this life on the road. He doesn't seem like a guy to stay in a place for long, I think, and the thought tugs at me.

When we're finished eating, I insist on clearing the plates away and washing up.

"Come out here," Beau calls as I'm finishing.

There's a ladder attached to the side of Bertha, and he's waiting to hoist me up.

I clamber up, intrigued. He's laid out some camping mats and a couple of blankets and pillows.

"I like to come up here in the evenings," he says, throwing himself down carelessly.

I drop down beside him, wrap my arms around my knees, feeling a little awkward.

But when he reaches for me, I tumble into his embrace easily. He lays me down on the pillows and wraps the blankets around us.

I shiver against him in delight.

"Cold?" He pulls the blankets up beneath my chin.

"Not anymore," I say. Hesitantly, I lift an arm and lay it across his chest. I'm shy to touch him like this. Despite everything we did this evening, we're still strangers. But Beau lays his hand over mine and gives a sigh of contentment, and it just feels *right*. Like we fit together perfectly.

He's so much bigger than me. So powerful and fierce, but I feel safe in his arms. I shuffle a little closer, Beau holds me more tightly, and I lay my head on his shoulder. Bliss. Pure bliss.

"Look up at the stars," he growls in my ear.

They're dazzling. It's a perfect, clear night. No moon, no clouds. Just thousands and thousands of stars scattered across the sky. I feel like I can see deep into the galaxies.

He chuckles at my exclamations of awe, and his thumb chafes my palm. I feel him trace the hard calluses that sit at the base of each finger.

Then he lifts my hand up and examines it. "These hands have done a lot of hard work," he comments.

"I was one of the launderers."

He turns his head sharply. "Money launderers?"

I giggle. "You really have no idea how simple my pack is. No, as in, it was my job to wash everyone's clothes."

He raises an eyebrow. "You mean by hand?"

"Yup. In the river. Pounding them with stones."

He tilts his head toward the little river tinkling in the distance. "That's why you—" He gives a shudder. "No. Just no. That's why god invented laundromats."

"He did?" I play along.

"Yup, on the eighth day, along with a ton of other stuff, so folks could concentrate on more important things."

"I've never even seen a laundromat. I'm ridiculous, aren't I?"

His voice turns so serious, it startles me. "Don't ever say that about yourself." He presses my hand to his lips and kisses it. "You're a princess. Don't you know that? You were born to be cherished. Protected. Not forced to operate a stone-age laundry service." His eyes are fierce, angry.

Princess? I can't breathe. My own eyes prickle.

He looks worried. "What is it?"

"On the territory, I used to get called *halfling* or *runt* all the time. I was part of the serving class. The omegas. The farthest thing from a princess, believe me."

A growl breaks from his throat. I whimper, pull away reflexively.

"Oh, I'm sorry." He chuckles and draws me in again. "I get a little protective sometimes." He strokes my hair, making soft, hushing sounds, until I calm.

"What happened, right before you left?" he asks gently.

I'm so embarrassed, but I tell him. All about the public nakedness and humiliation.

He looks even angrier than before, and he grits his teeth. I sense he's struggling to keep his wolf down.

When I'm done, he says, "they didn't deserve you, Little One. Thank goodness your mom brought you here, so you can start living the life you deserve."

Does he mean with him? I can't look at him. Instead, I stare up at the starry sky, a sick, excitable lurch in my stomach. I'm so confused. I already know I want to be with him, always. But I don't know what that means. I'm so ignorant of the world outside of the pack. Does he have a harem somewhere, where he keeps his mates? Is he going to let me fall for him, then abandon me when he gets tired of me?

Beau lays a gentle finger on my cheek. I turn my head to him again, and he's right there, his soft, firm lips, seeking out my own.

He's gentle at first. Holding me in his arms, while his lips draw my soul out from my body. I feel like we're levitating together, wrapped in a blanket, but lifted up, up into the starry sky, racing toward eternity. My eyes are closed, but constellations sparkle behind my eyelids.

Soon, his kisses become more urgent, his velvety tongue plunging deeper into my mouth. I cling to him, yearning for him to possess me, to make me his.

With a growl, he flips me onto my back and arches over me. His strong, muscular thighs push between mine, spreading my legs apart. Instinctively, I lift them up, around him, and I feel his cock, already hard, pressing against my core. That big, hard bulge, rubbing back and forth against my aching clit. Already, I'm wet again. All I can think about is how much I want him inside me. That big, beautiful cock taking my virginity.

But when I reach for it, he snatches my hand away. "Savannah," he growls, low in his throat.

Confusion burns. "What? Y-you don't really want me?"

He gives a tortured groan. "You don't understand how much I want to take your virginity right now. Claim that sweet little pussy of yours. But I can't."

"I'm ready," I tell him. "I want you to take me now. I don't care what happens tomorrow. I just need you, right here."

With a ragged sigh, he presses his hand against my pussy. "So wet, so ready for me," he murmurs.

"So, what are you waiting for?"

"My wolf—" he breaks off, doesn't finish the sentence.

"What?"

"I can't take a mate," he says at last.

I blink fast, trying to grasp his meaning. "You've never had a mate?"

"Nope." He is looking down at me, tenderly, wistfully.

My heart beats fast. "In your whole life?"

"I thought I met my mate when I was young, younger than most. But it didn't work out."

"And now?"

"Oh, right now, I want to fuck you more than I've wanted anything in the whole world. But I'm scared my wolf will destroy us both."

"B-but—" I stutter. "Why would it if you want this?"

"I was wrong before." He looks so sad, it pierces my heart. "If I'm wrong again, I won't make it out this time. Because there's no knowing what my wolf would do."

"Why would you be wrong?" Ridiculously, my lip trembles. I like him so much, and I can't stand the thought that I might make him sick somehow.

"Because I don't trust it anymore."

I hardly dare speak the words. "What does it tell you?"

He gives a low growl. "It says you're mine. It's been saying that ever since you opened those beautiful green eyes of yours and looked at me."

"I feel the same," I manage to say.

"You do?"

"When you pulled me out of the riverbank, I felt like I'd been struck by lightning."

"You're mine, little wolf, I feel it deep in my bones," he murmurs, his voice low and husky. "But I fear the fates. I fear I wasn't destined to understand them."

"What happened last time?" Jealousy burns inside me. I don't want to hear about him being intimate with another female. But I have to know.

He sighs, draws away from me and lies on his back again, staring up at the sky.

"My wolf is a difficult one," he says, after a pause so long I thought he wasn't going to answer.

I close my eyes, buffeted by this torrent of fire and ice. His cock still hard, ready for me. And I sense his need, crackling through his body like electricity.

He's into me, but he hates that he's into me? I'm so confused.

"WE'D BETTER GET you to bed," he says.

I sit up, pushing off the blanket, and a breeze whips up, chilling me all the way through. I'm bone tired. It's been a long, long day.

I follow Beau down from the roof. He helps me descend the steps, his hands warm on my hips. The way he touches me—it's like his hands were made for me.

Inside the bus, he pulls on a handle on the wall, and a narrow bed springs down, set on some ingenious contraption. He lays a pillow and comforter on top.

"There you go," he says. Then he rummages around in a cupboard and pulls out a bunch of canvas and poles. "I'll be right outside if you need anything."

"You're not sleeping here?" I mumble, drowsy, confused.

He gives a dry laugh, as if that's a crazy idea. Maybe it is. I'm not sure if I'd be able to sleep with him beside me. "No. I'll be in my tent."

"I can't kick you out of your bed."

"My wolf likes sleeping outside. Night, Savannah. Sweet dreams."

He shuts the door, and I'm alone inside Bertha.

I wash up, then slide beneath the comforter. The pillow smells of him—his spicy, exciting masculine scent—and desire shudders through me yet again.

I turn onto my back. I don't understand men. I wish my mom had told me about their complexities and contradictions, instead of just warning me about the ugliness and suffering under their brutal harems.

7

Beau

Outside, I dump the tent underneath the bus. My animal is raging beneath my skin, burning me up inside.

Having that sweet little she-wolf in my arms drove me to the limits of my sanity. I shouldn't have touched her earlier. And I definitely shouldn't have kissed her just now, shouldn't have gotten hard again.

My wolf and I are at war.

She's mine.

All I want is to claim her.

I've been hoping I could take care of her. Protect her. Keep her safe. And that could be enough.

But she drives my wolf wild.

Of course, she does. She's the hottest darn thing I've

seen in my entire life. And every part of me insists, she's the one.

I thought I was destined for loneliness.

But Savannah and I complete each other.

She's the one my wolf has been craving all these years.

I hated that I couldn't tell her the truth. I've never spoken the words aloud for fear of what it'll do to my wolf. I've worked hard to suppress even the memories. To compartmentalize them in my rational half, keep them safe from my wild half.

And the past day has been a taste of what will happen to my animal if it experiences a rejection again.

I CAST a glance at the small town in the distance. A few lights twinkle from buildings, but looks like most people are asleep already.

I strip my clothes off and let my wolf come. It needs a release; it's the only way I'll be able to keep it under control all night long.

It bursts out of me, eager to be the one in charge. Silently, I make a deal with it:

Run now for as long as you want, so long as you quit tearing me up inside.

My wolf is not always one to honor a deal, I think wryly. Remembering those mad years in the forest, trapped within my beastly form.

Concealed beneath a blanket of darkness, I run along the riverbank. There's little chance of being seen here. Might encounter a solitary, nocturnal fisherman or two, but I'll smell them coming from a mile away.

I run for miles and miles, out of Perdue Town, into another small town and then another. I pass two lovers kissing on a bridge, too wrapped up in each other to notice a big gray wolf intruding on civilization. I pass three fisherman crouching in the darkness, their equipment illuminated by little electric lamps. I pick up the scent of a rabbit, give chase, and snatch it up in my jaws. I'm not really hungry, but the thrill of the chase, followed by the satisfying taste of freshly hunted meat calms my wolf. Make things right in its world.

I run until I'm tired, and then I turn and go back home. By the time the reassuring bulk of Bertha comes into view, my paws are sore. We must've been out a couple of hours. I trot up to the door of the van and listen for Savannah. The sound of slow, regular breathing washes comfort into my bones. She's sleeping deeply, poor thing. She must be exhausted.

Satisfied that she's safe, I bound up the ladder and make myself comfortable up on the roof. The wind has whipped up and no way am I fiddling with tent pegs and ropes on the riverbank.

At last, my wolf is exhausted, and I sleep.

* * *

WHEN MY EYES snap open again, the sky is still pure black and glittering with stars. But a terrible racket fills my ears. Banging, wailing, snarling. I lurch upright, electricity charging my body.

Savannah.

In a single bound, I crash all the way down to the ground, then I tear open the door of the bus, and—

The interior is in chaos. Things knocked over, broken. The bed overturned. And in the midst of it all is a small, silver she-wolf. Standing in the middle of the floor, trembling and whimpering.

Her wolf. My heart soars. Small, soft, her first shift. But I see strength in those glowing green eyes of hers.

At the sight of me, she freezes, then she whines in relief. I bound over to her and lick her soft muzzle, reassuring her that everything's okay. Little by little, the trembling stops.

I lead her out of the van and make her follow me. I want her to enjoy this, her first shift. It's an important moment for any wolf. We run a couple of laps around the bus and I watch her get accustomed to her new form, running faster and faster, reveling in the strength of her four legs. Then I snap at her playfully, and we tussle a little. She yaps in excitement, leaping all over me. I see how her wolf submits to mine when I make a dominant gesture, and it's a beautiful, endearing sight.

When we're safely back inside, I shift, and she watches me avidly. Then I tell her to shift as well. "Let your human form return," I tell her. "Relax and will it to happen."

It doesn't come easy. She whines and her body thrashes like she's wrestling with a snake. "Relax, take your time," I keep telling her, making my voice soft and encouraging.

Then it happens. There's a loud snap, a series of

cracks, and she shoots upright. There's my girl again, standing on two feet and gloriously naked.

"Oh, my god," she gasps out and burst into tears. She's shaking all over, her chest heaving with sobs.

I snatch her up, take her in my arms. "Hush, it's okay, honey," I murmur. "You just had your first shift. This is real good news."

"I was s-so scared," she stutters in between sobs. "I was sleeping, and I woke up and this was happening. It was terrible. I couldn't control it. She half burst out of me, and I was smashing all around the van. Trashing all of your nice stuff."

My heart blooms with tenderness. "Don't worry about my stuff," I say. "You're the important thing here." I keep muttering soothing words and stroking her back.

At last, she draws back and looks up into my face. "My wolf came," she says, and there's a sense of wonder in her voice now. "I thought she would never come. I was a halfling who couldn't shift. And now it's happened."

I stroke her soft cheek, wondering if it wasn't such a coincidence that it happened today.

She frowns. "But will it always be like this? All violent and scary?"

"No." I chuckle. "Of course not. It's just weird because it was the first time. Next time will be better and the time after. And after that, it'll be second nature. You'll see."

She takes a big breath, and her chest swells, which has the effect of pushing her beautiful bare breasts closer to me. "Thank you, Beau," she says, and her eyes turn soft and dreamy.

Before I know it, I'm dipping my head to her, and we're kissing again. Her lush naked body touches mine, and as her velvety tongue touches against mine, my cock turns hard as a rock. Naked, there's no hiding it, and it presses against her soft belly.

She pulls back and looks at it in amazement. She makes a little sound of awe, and the sweet fragrance of her arousal rises to my nostrils. I try to control myself, but before long, my hands are running all over her creamy skin, cupping her lovely round tits and chafing those sweet nipples. And then she wraps her soft little hand around my cock, and I'm lost. A growl of need bursts from my throat. All I can think about is how tight her sweet pussy felt earlier. How much I need to be inside her, to mate her. To claim her for my own.

"Savannah—" I manage to say, and I tear her hand away.

"What?" She's bolder this time, and she runs her other hand up and down my aching shaft. "Beau, I need you inside me."

"I can't." I grit out between clenched teeth.

She gives a huff of disappointment. Then those green eyes of hers sparkle with wickedness. "Then I'm going to make you feel good, like you made me earlier."

Her hand is still moving up and down, and I lack the self-control to pull it away this time. My breathing comes rough and heavy, with my nose full of her smell and her tiny hand driving me to distraction.

"Just like earlier," she repeats, lethal intention blazing in her eyes.

"What—? No," I protest, but it's too late. Before I truly grasp what's happening, my beautiful little she-wolf has dropped to her knees and she's pressing her lips to the swollen head of my cock. When her tongue flicks across the tip, she gives a sweet sigh.

Then she opens her mouth and starts to take it in. I swear my feet leave the ground.

Too late to stop her now. *As if I had the self-control to do that anyway.* Instead, I surrender my will and enjoy the sight of those sweet cherry lips around my dick. That blissed-out, unearthly sensation of sliding into her warm mouth. Her soft tongue licking my most sensitive place while sounds of enjoyment escape her lips. I slide in and out a little, marveling at how she can take me, my fierce little she-wolf.

But too soon, I'm approaching crisis point. "Savannah, stop," I mutter.

But she understands; she grabs my ass in both her hands and keeps going.

Fuck.

My hands move to grab her head and I snatch them away again. "Savannah."

My knees go weak. I start to shake all over. My cock surges, and I'm coming in her soft mouth. My hot seed spilling into her. Euphoria burns through me as she swallows me so sweetly.

Then she sits back on her knees, licking her lips. This beautiful princess.

"You shouldn't have done that," I mutter, pulling her to her feet and holding her tight.

"Oh, I wanted to," she says, and there's something new in her voice now. The voice of a woman who knows exactly what she wants. Her pussy presses against my thigh, riding it and I feel how wet she is.

"Did you like that?" I growl.

She groans in response. I slide my hand down and cup her drenched pussy. Her clit jolts beneath my finger. Beautiful swollen bud. Carefully I slide a finger inside her. There's barely space for it. "So tight, Little One," I croon, and she gasps.

"I want to take that virginity of yours. Push my cock inside your tight little pussy."

"You don't want it," she mutters.

"Oh, you don't understand how much I do."

"Feel those little muscles of yours gripping my cock so tight."

"Shove myself all the way inside you."

"Make you come until you beg me to stop."

She groans and sighs at each filthy word I growl in her ear, while I work her little pussy with my fingers.

I feel her getting close, her body shaking.

She rides her clit on the heel of my hand. Her breath catches, she stops breathing altogether... and she gives a sharp cry and spasms around my finger. I feel her orgasm pulsing all the way through her sweet body. It's an amazing thing.

"You're beautiful," I tell her, when I finally slide my finger out of her.

I lead her to the bed and straighten it up before laying her down.

"Will you stay with me?" she murmurs sleepily.

"I don't know, darlin'."

"If you're not going to fuck me, at least sleep with me," she murmurs.

I slide in next to her. Wrap her soft body with mine.

Before long, her breathing turns soft and regular, and she slumps in my arms. This little angel, her dark eyelashes splayed across her cheeks. I watch her for a long time, see the tiny movements of her eyelids as she dreams, and I hope with all my heart that they're happy dreams.

Sleep doesn't come for me. Having Savannah's soft curves in my arms is pure torment. My wolf is hella antsy. Pacing inside me. Making its demands. Not *understanding*. Every time she snuggles closer, I clench my fists and grit my teeth, fighting it down. And whenever I start to drift, she gives a sleepy sigh, and I'm wide awake again.

Pure torment.

I don't care though; I love holding her in my arms and keeping her safe. This pleasure I can allow myself.

At last, the stars fade, and sunrise brightens the eastern sky. The night is almost over, and I'm still awake. Watching the morning light kissing her skin.

Annihilated.

8

Savannah

I wake up to bright daylight. The space beside me is empty, but when I lay my hand on the sheet, it still carries a hint of Beau's warmth. His smell. Every time I woke up during the night, he was there. His muscular bulk curved around me. Protecting me.

Last night floods back, and my body wakes up, desire licking at my skin, wrapping itself around my limbs.

It wasn't supposed to happen. He kept pushing me away.

But then it did.

I pleasured him, took his big, beautiful cock in my mouth. And I made him come. This big, powerful alpha climaxed in my mouth, legs trembling, groaning out my name like it was a precious jewel.

I felt strong, wild, sexy. I felt like *his.*

I'm still terrified of mating. Those awful sounds I heard on the territory still echo in my head. But my desire for Beau is stronger. I need him inside me like I need to breathe.

Still, he won't take me.

Keeps saying his wolf is a *difficult one.*

Whatever that means.

I reach for my phone, check the time.

Then I leap out of bed like I've been electrocuted. Somehow the alarm didn't go off, and I was supposed to be at work a half hour ago. *Crap, crap, crap.*

I cast around for my clothes. Find a few scraps in the corners of the room. They got shredded when I had my first shift last night. *Double crap.* I yank the sheet off the bed, wrap it around me and burst outside.

And I stop dead. Because there's Beau, sitting at the table, in nothing but a pair of shorts. His dark hair hangs wet around his face and his beautiful golden torso glistens with water droplets.

My golden river god.

My breath shudders in my throat as I take him in.

He's busy, working at a laptop and he doesn't look up right away.

My heart hammers because I have no idea what he's thinking now. If he's regretting last night. If he's about to say something that'll bring my whole world crashing down.

"I'm late for work," I announce.

Now he raises his head and breaks into a grin. "So happens I changed your shift for you."

I stumble down the steps. "You did?"

"Yup. I figured we'd go shopping this morning. You're on at five p.m. instead."

"S-shopping?" I stutter.

He eyes the sheet that's wrapping my body. "By my reckoning you're down to one set of clothes, and to be honest with you, they're not exactly in the best shape."

Okay. He's got a point. If I go to a discount store, I should be able to buy a whole new outfit with yesterday's earnings, I calculate. Maybe a couple of sets of underwear, too.

"Don't you worry about money, darlin'," he says. "I've got plenty."

I plant my hands on my hips. "I can't take your money, Beau. You've done more than enough for me already."

His grin gets wider. "To tell you the truth, I've got more money than I know what to do with. My needs are small." He throws a glance at Bertha. "I donate a bunch of it to various charities that take care of disadvantaged kids. The rest of it is just sitting in my bank account doing nothing. Can't think of anything I'd rather do with it, than get your sweet body dressed up in the way you deserve. Now go get yourself ready, and I'll fix you something to eat. Then we're going shopping."

Is it wrong of me to be so excited? I hurry through my shower, my tummy tingling. I've never been taken shopping in my life. Hell, I've never had brand-new clothes before. All our clothes came from Goodwill. Werewolves who live in packs don't think a ton about their clothes. I dry off fast and pull my old things on, hoping I'll be in time to help Beau in the kitchen. He's halfway done, but I make the toast and pour the coffee. We lay everything out at the table, and he takes his seat with a contented sigh.

"Isn't this the life?" he says, his blue eyes catching the morning light as he gazes out at the sparkling river.

I wish that every day could start like this; me and Beau sitting beside Bertha, eating our breakfast, full of simple appreciation for the nature around us.

Just for this moment, I like to believe there's magic in the air, in the water. This little supermarket parking lot feels like paradise. I'm no longer an unwanted halfling, but the mate of the river god.

I'm still wondering how we're going to go shopping, when a throaty roar starts up from the far side of Bertha and Beau tears around the corner on his stylish black motorcycle. A café racer, he calls it.

"We're going on your bike?" I say stupidly.

"Sure are." He flashes that sexy grin of his and hands me a helmet.

I fumble it on, and he helps me, fastening the chin-strap snugly under my chin. "Sit close," he tells me. "Hold tight to my waist. And don't be scared. A werewolf's reflexes are faster than lightning."

I nod, knowing he's right.

I think I'm prepared for the speed, but it still startles

me as he weaves in and out of the traffic. I wrap my arms around his muscular waist, and grip with my thighs as the wind blasts past us. Every time we stop at a traffic light, he checks in, squeezes my hand reassuringly, and I stop feeling scared. I know he'd never let me come to any harm.

WHEN HE PULLS into a shopping mall, I gawp at it like the little hick I am. I've only seen these in movies before.

Beau takes my hand, leads me along while I stumble, overwhelmed by all the new sights. My head swivels this way and that. So much choice; so many fashion stores full of clothes so much prettier than anything I've owned before.

He looks around a little dazedly, rubbing at his hair. Guess he's not used to female fashions, either.

"Let's start here." He points to a store. It looks real fancy.

"I don't know—" I start to say.

He picks out a real pretty outfit in the window. "Think that'd look perfect on you."

When I protest, he drags me inside.

He takes charge, picking out outfits, asking the shop assistants for advice. They fawn over him, batting their eyelashes. Every woman has the hots for him. Jealousy surges in me, and I feel embarrassed being in the store with all these nice things, all the other girls dressed appropriately, when what I'm wearing is basically one step up from rags. To make things worse, my wolf keeps growling possessively. Now she's woken up, I can't get her to go back to sleep.

Beau leads me to the dressing room, and gets an assistant to lay out all the clothes for me.

"Now, go in there and try everything on," he tells me.

A thrill goes through me as I stumble in and pull the curtains shut. I kind of like it when he's bossy like this. Like it more than I should.

I pull on one outfit after another, tear back the curtain and show him.

Beau likes the things that cling tight to my curves, emphasize my rounded hips and big boobs. I'm usually real self-conscious about them, but I feel myself blossoming through his compliments. Try to see myself as the sexy woman he insists I am.

By the time we're done, I have three new pairs of jeans, two dresses, and a bunch of shirts and lingerie. The assistants pack them so prettily in tissue paper with little bows and stickers, before handing them over in expensive bags. Beau insists on carrying everything, and all I can do is wander along, holding his hand, feeling like a princess in a movie. He insists I get a bunch of nice toiletries, too, and a hairdryer and a new backpack.

When we're finally done, he looks at his watch.

"Just time to have lunch before I need to get you to work," he says. "What do you want to eat?"

We go to a food court, and I'm like a kid in a candy store. Burgers, tacos, pizza. All these things I've read about in books or seen in movies. All these things for other people, not a feral girl from a savage pack. My stomach is rumbling, but I can't decide.

"You're overwhelmed, aren't you, honey?" Beau says, his eyes tender. In the end, he winds up ordering burgers, quesadillas, hotdogs and strawberry shakes for us both. It's too much food, but I savor every delicious mouthful.

"THANK YOU. That was the best day ever," I say, as he fits all my things into the pannier on his bike and we climb back on.

"The pleasure was all mine," he says, and his eyes crinkle at the corners. "It was worth it to see you looking so happy."

He's a dream. An absolute dream, I think as we pull up in front of the bar. Soon, I'm going to wake up and find I'm still sleeping in a filthy riverbed, and this whole thing was a product of my poor, delirious mind.

I expect Beau to roar off again, but he shuts off the engine and strolls inside the bar with me. He looks around, takes a seat in the farthest corner. "I'm just gonna work here for a while," he says. "You won't even know I'm here."

NOT TRUE.

All night long, Beau's presence blazes through me like wildfire. My eyes keep drifting to his ruggedly handsome face. Every nerve in my body cries out for him. I long to feel the sexy scrape of his beard against my skin. His firm, plush lips crashing against my own.

Those big, callused hands wrapping around my body. Possessing me.

Now I understand what he means when he says his wolf is *a difficult one*—he's warning me not to fall in love with him.

But it's too late.

I've already given him my heart.

* * *

TWO MORE DAYS pass like this.

Beau takes a copy of my roster and Meredith's, and he watches me when she's not around. She grumbles, but I think she's secretly glad he's there. A free security service.

Because there are a lot of shady characters on these streets, shuffling in, looking for people who don't want to be found. But one look at Beau, and they never come back again.

He's leaving his scent all around town.

Letting everyone know he's with me.

"He's a real possessive one, that man of yours," Meredith comments. Her elbows are propped up on the bar, eyes lingering on Beau's broad shoulders and tight buns as he leaves to run an errand.

"He's not mine," I say.

She slides me a sideways look. "Not from where I'm standing, hun." She sighs luxuriously. "I'd kill for a guy like that."

So would I. Because he's not mine.

. . .

AFTER WORK, Beau brings me home and we have dinner, watching the sun go down or staring up at the stars. And we talk. He asks me everything about my life before him, my dreams for the future. I didn't even know I had dreams until he teased them out. I told him how I liked to make little handicrafts and sell them at the local market. When I told him how much I was selling them for, he shook his head in disbelief and pulled out his laptop. Turns out there are Internet sites where you can sell them for five times the price.

"You make 'em, I'll get them sold for you," he says.

He encourages and probes me until I admit I always wanted to make clothes, and he says he'll get me a sewing machine and all the things I need to go with it. I can take a course to learn the techniques.

It's pure bliss here—just him, me and our little bus. And all these dreams I never dared entertain before.

Except he hasn't so much as kissed me since that first night. He barely even touches me.

And it's driving me insane.

My panties are soaking wet, all the time. My nipples ache, hell, my clit throbs. I feel like a cat on heat. Hungry for him, and only him.

And the worst part is, I know he feels the same. I catch the yearning in those fierce blue eyes when I come down the steps in the morning; see his cock swelling beneath his zipper.

But he pushes it away.

Ever since that first night, he's insisted on sleeping outside. And sometimes I hear his wolf prowling around. Feral, anguished.

Suffering.

How long before this gets too much for Beau and he leaves me?

My wolf howls at the thought.

I think she'd curl up and die if he left me.

9

Beau

Every day, my wolf is getting sicker.

I had a plan—

I'd stay with Savannah until she was earning enough to get her own little place. The independence she always talks of. She doesn't want my money. I told her jokingly that I've got enough in the bank to support a whole harem of women. Of course, it was a joke. Because the only one I want is her. But she hated it. Her face went pale, and I felt like the biggest asshole in the universe. I apologized until she forgave me. I wonder what else went on with her pack. She's not real forthcoming about it. I get the impression she'd rather not think about any of it again.

—If Savannah gets her own place—then what? I'll watch her from a distance.

Let her take another mate?

Over my dead body, my wolf roars.

I thought if I didn't touch her, it'd keep the beast in check. But all this frustration seems to be making it worse. It's feral, aggressive. Whenever I lose focus, it tries to burst out of me, to take control. And the only thing that scares me more than this is the thought of losing Savannah altogether.

ONE MORNING, I drop Savannah off at work. She's quieter than usual, while most of my attention is going into keeping the beast in check. Trying hard not to notice how hot her ass looks, jiggling in her new skinny jeans.

I hold the door of the bar open for her, and half-way through, she stops and turns to me. Her sweet cherry lips are inches from my face, and that familiar wave of sweet-sick desire floods me. I long to dip my head and claim them. But right now, they're pale and pinched at the edges.

"You don't need to watch me today, Beau," she tells me.

I frown. "Of course, I do."

"I need to stand on my own two feet."

A dart of unease pierces my chest. "What do you mean?"

"I mean, I can't spend my life being guarded." Her lower lip trembles. "I want to work alone today."

"But I need to keep you safe."

"Beau, please."

I study her a moment longer, trying to interpret the emotions at war in her eyes. I want to insist. Know I don't have the right.

I exhale slowly. "Okay, then. I'll come pick you up when you're done."

She shakes her head. "I'll make my own way home, Beau."

"It's not safe—"

She lays her soft hand on my chest. "I can't live like this."

My head spins. "Being protected?"

"Yeah. Yeah, I guess that's what I mean." She stalks through the door and disappears into the bar.

Automatically, I move to go after her. To my wolf, there's an invisible leash that connects me to her. It can't stand to be too far away.

But at the last second, I stop myself. There was something new in her expression, and I sense that if I push myself onto her right now, I'll break her trust.

Instead, I turn around and reorient myself toward the little café on the opposite side of the street. Nothing wrong with watching her if she doesn't know I'm there.

Inside, I grab a double Americano and settle myself into a seat by the window, which gives me a good view of Sinners'.

I open my laptop and try to focus on my work— investigating the offshore accounts of a political hopeful, but every couple of minutes, my eyes drift to the window. I wonder what Savannah is doing right now. If she's happier than she was when I left her. The thought turns like a screw in my chest. I want to make her the happiest person alive. She deserves that and so much more, but I only seem to be making her sad.

Halfway through the morning, the door of the bar opens and my attention focuses in, like a heat-seeking missile.

A familiar figure exits, stalks across the street, and throws open the door of the café. In another second, she's right by my table, elbows jutting out, beady eyes scrutinizing me like a worm she's about to yank out of the earth.

"You're not supposed to be here!" she shrills, planting her elbows on her bony hips.

I wince. "Good morning to you, too, Elinor."

She wags her finger at me. "You're not being very nice to my friend."

I swallow hard. "What do you mean?"

"She's sad. And I don't like my friends to be sad."

"I'm trying to protect her!"

Her birdy eyes narrow to little black slits. "Who from?"

I take a deep, ruminative breath. "Myself."

"Yourself?" Her eyes bulge. "That's crazy talk. Anyone can see she's smitten with you."

"She is?" My heart seems to skip a beat.

"Of course."

"My wolf—" I break off, unsure how to explain.

Elinor bends at the waist and peers into my face. I push my wolf way down, as it's longing to snap at her, and I hold still and let her do her thing.

Her eyelids flicker like an information processing device. "You struggle with it, huh?" she says at last.

I blink, surprised at this bird-brain's perspicacity. "I do."

"Better fix it." She wags her finger at me again. "Or you'll lose her forever."

She turns on her heel and sasses her way out of the café.

I DROP my head into my hands. I was trying to doing my best for Savannah, protecting her, keeping her safe, even as I fought all my instincts to take her, make her mine.

But all this time I've been hurting her. Kissing her, giving her orgasms, then refusing to mate her. Probably making her feel rejected again, which is the last thing I ever wanted.

I thought I was doing the right thing, but I'm starting to think I'll hurt her less by being out of her life altogether.

Being away from her will kill me.

But I can't stand for her to hurt anymore.

I push back my chair.

A moment later, I'm out the door, too.

* * *

I DASH ALL the way back to Bertha. Then I grab a notepad, scrawl out a note.

Savannah, I need to go away on a job for a couple of days.

I'll be back soon—

I hesitate. Because the truth is, I might not be back. I might fall into a place so dark there's no way out. Instead, I write:

Bertha is yours now. Please make her your home.

Stay safe.

My hand trembles at the last bit:

All my love,

Beau.

Before I can change my mind, I tape it to the door, jump onto my bike, and roar off. And I don't look back, because if I did, I wouldn't be able to leave.

Elinor was right. I can't go on like this anymore. My animal is so close to the surface the whole time, I feel like a million fire ants are crawling over my skin. It's all I can do to keep it under control. It needs a release. But I'm terrified that once it's out, it might not go back in again. The memory of the sickness, of those two years of pain and grieving while I was trapped in its wolf form, washes through me yet again.

I know what I'm risking. There's a good chance I won't make it back.

But Savannah is worth every bit of pain and suffering.

And if I don't do this, I'll lose her altogether.

On the way, I pull over, message Meredith and ask her to keep an eye on Savannah.

She'll be safe in the town. I've prowled every inch of it, shown every asshole—shifter and human alike—that she's under my protection.

She messages me right back:

Do what you need to. But you better come back

A wry smile tugs at my lips. If I'm not around to watch Savannah, she's the next best thing. She's a wise bear; she understands how screwed up some of us are.

A HALF HOUR LATER, I arrive at my destination. I ride in, as deep as I can. And then I strip off and release my wolf.

And I pray this isn't the last time I'll know my human form.

10

Savannah

*H*e's gone. He's really gone.

When I peel off the note he taped to the door of the bus, the words blur from the tears that spill from my eyes.

Because I know, deep in my heart that he hasn't just gone away on a job.

He's giving Bertha to me. And he's not coming back.

This thing I've been fearing ever since Beau didn't want to kiss me anymore has come true.

Darkness comes down over my vision, and I cling onto the side of the bus for support.

He's left me, because somehow, being with me hurts him.

I can't let this happen, I can't.

I burst into the cabin and rush around, searching, searching for any kind of clue about his whereabouts.

But there's nothing.

I tip my head back and howl.

And just like that, my wolf comes. I only have time to rip my jeans off, before she bursts out of me, tearing up every other thing I'm wearing.

Then she goes ballistic. Hurtling around the van, trashing the place, just like she did last time. She burns with anguish, calling for her mate again and again.

A long time passes before I can get her back under control.

AND WHEN I'M finally standing on two feet again, trembling, I discover she's torn up half the upholstery. Her teeth and claws are damned sharp.

As I look around in dismay, I realize I can't stay here. This lovely place that became a home to me. Yes, because it's a beautiful little house, but mostly because Beau was in it. And every last thing reminds me of him.

I guess he thought he was showing me a kindness, leaving Bertha to me. But I can't stand to see her. So, I grab a few things, lock up, and make my way back to the bar.

MEREDITH IS WAITING FOR ME. "Come here, honey," she says and enfolds me in her big, strong arms.

I won't cry, I won't cry, I tell myself as I lean into her embrace. She so soft, so enveloping. The mother I never had.

"He's left me, hasn't he?" I demand.

When she draws back, her brown eyes are bright with sympathy.

"That wolf of yours is a tortured soul. But he's also a real good man. Maybe he just needs a little time to himself."

"I'm not enough for him, am I?"

"Oh, honey, you're more than enough for him. The first time I saw him, sloping around here by himself, before he met you, I thought to myself, there goes a lonely, wounded soul."

I shake my head in disbelief.

She chuckles. "Oh, you don't see him that way, do you? Because he's all big and protective and tough. And he's all that, in spades. But he's also got a wound, a hole deep inside him, that goes all the way back to his early years." She lays a hand on her chest. "I've got a sense for these things."

"But how can I help him?" I almost laugh at my own words. Me, who's so naïve. So ignorant about the ways of the world. I've never even had sex before.

She shakes her head. "You've helped by being there. Ever since he brought you in that first day, he's been different. More himself. Easier in his own skin."

I blink fast, and my heart starts pounding like a jack-hammer. *Is that true? Have I really been good for him?* "But he still left me—" I mutter.

"Guess he's got something he needs to do first," she says. "You want my advice?"

I nod eagerly.

"Give him a little time. But be ready for him when he's done. You don't want to let that one go."

I go still, remembering that feeling I'd had—that we completed each other. In the last few days, I thought I'd lost it. But it's still there, like a candle flame, fighting to stay lit in a breeze.

I hold up my bag. "Is there anywhere from me to crash here?"

She puffs out her cheeks. "I'm as full as ever, but I'm sure you can get Birdbrain to share a bunk with you."

I break into a smile. My heart might be torn in two, but I'm lucky to have Meredith as a surrogate mother and a hectic little crow as a best friend.

ELINOR ISN'T JUST happy to share her bunk with me. She insists on throwing a pajama party—the first one I've ever had. She gives me one of her spare sets, and introduces me to all her roomies. When the bar is closed, we sneak downstairs and make popcorn in the kitchen. Then we stay up late, hiding under the comforter and gossiping.

I don't hear from Beau that night, or the next. Every hour that passes without him turns another knot in my stomach. When I think of him, I sense his pain and grief. A darkness pulling him down. I feel it like it's my own pain, and my soul cries out to him.

But my wolf is becoming unbearable, clawing at me, howling for me to go to my mate. She's making things a ton worse. I need to forget that I ever thought Beau could be mine. It's the only way I'll survive.

* * *

THE THIRD DAY dawns stormy and gray, the rain pelting down outside. And something in me shifts.

He's been gone long enough.

The thought arrives in my heart, fully formed.

I slip out of bed, trying not to wake Elinor, who's snoring softly on the pillow beside me, and I creep downstairs.

I've got to go and get him.

The notion blazes in my brain like a neon sign, and it gets more and more dazzling as I leave the bar. Rain is falling heavily, bouncing off the sidewalk. I pull my jacket over my head and go faster, faster, until I'm sprinting across the deserted town all the way back to Bertha.

The plan wasn't fully fleshed out, but now I'm here, I know there's only one thing I can do.

Bertha sits there, waiting for me so patiently. Our little home.

I climb into the driver's seat and put the key in the ignition. She starts up immediately with a soft purr. The engine works perfectly—of course, it does. I scan the controls. I don't have a license, but I used to drive a truck to the market and back. I think I know what I'm doing. Of course, driving an old school bus is different from a pick-up. But the brake and the gas and the gear-stick seem to all work the same. I steer a lap around the parking lot, checking I know what I'm doing, then off we go.

I drive alongside the river, heading north, purely because it feels right. Beau went off to fix himself, or lose his mind, I'm not sure which. Where would a shifter who's struggling with their animal go?

After I've been driving for an hour or so, I see a turn off for Devil's Den state forest. I take it. The only thing directing me is my instinct, but I feel it as true as an arrow in my heart. Just like I feel that I'm coming closer to Beau with every step.

I follow the signs to a parking lot. Trails continue past it, but I figure I can't go any farther with a bulky school bus. Instead, I park up.

Then I strip off and shift—because that's the only thing that will help me right now. My wolf springs out of me with a joyous bark. I don't need to think any more, I just let her run.

And she's off, galloping, her aim never faltering as she dashes among the endless trees. Her paws churn up the earth, and she pants with exhilaration, nose twitching, desperate to pick up his scent.

The forest gets darker, barely any daylight filtering through the dense canopy of trees. It feels like a lonely, forlorn place. I understand why it's called Devil's Den. But suddenly, there's a man—coming through the trees. Dark hair hanging loose around his face, a black beard covering his jaws. Tall, muscular, and gloriously naked.

With a yap of joy, my wolf hurtles toward him—

Then skids to a stop, inches away.

Because he looks feral, nothing like the Beau I know.

His eyes are blazing with a strange light, and his face is drawn with torment.

My wolf yips in alarm, while my heart hurts for him. He's suffering.

He frowns, dipping his head among the shadows to see me better. "Savannah?"

I give an answering bark.

Damn. I need to regain my human form, but my wolf won't relinquish it easily. I push hard at her, calling her back inside me.

There's a series of cracks and crunches, and at last I stand naked in front of Beau in the middle of the forest.

"Here I am," I say, and I hold my arms loose at my sides. Not embarrassed or humiliated as I was before. But ready for whatever will come. Because now I know I'm worthy of a good mate. I understand that Beau has protected me all this time. And that he didn't run away because he didn't like me enough.

"You came." His white teeth flash in the dimness of the forest.

With a deep growl, he takes one more step towards me, and I'm in his arms. He draws me up, lifting me right off my feet, and he kisses me fiercely, his mouth crashing against mine. Relief sweeps through me and I open to him, welcoming him in. Wanting him to take all of me.

After a long time, he puts me down on the forest floor, but stays close, holding both my hands. "You came," he says again.

"I couldn't leave you alone out here," I say simply.

"You were brave." His thick brows knit together.

"Thought I was going to lose control of my beast for good."

"But why?"

"A long time ago, I went feral for two whole years. Lived in the wilderness, trapped inside my beast. All crazed and destructive. Felt like it was going to happen again."

"What happened to you, Beau?" I say softly, knowing his words won't come easily.

His massive chest rises, and I hear him take a ragged breath. "I thought I met my mate when I was young. We grew up together. And I just assumed... thought that was enough. But when we came of age, she chose another. An enemy of mine. Just about drove my wolf insane. I almost destroyed my pack—" He breaks off, takes several more slow breaths. "It's been... difficult ever since. That's why I've had to live alone all these years, never getting too close to anyone. It took all my control to keep my wolf at bay, stop it from going feral."

I gather myself, sympathy and jealousy warring in my chest.

"But you're not like that anymore—"

Something shifts in his eyes. They're his usual cornflower blue again, but full of ferocity.

"No, I'm not. But I'll be that and much more to protect you, Savannah. You're mine, and nothing is going to get in the way of that again."

Butterflies flutter in my stomach. "You want to be with me?"

He lets off a groan of anguish. "Of course. You're my mate. I've known that since the first moment I saw you."

I bite my lip. I can't believe I'm about to ask such an egotistical question. "With your last mate, did you feel like...like you'd been struck by lightning around her?" My cheeks burn.

His gaze turns fierce again. "No, not once. I was naïve then, still a kid. I had no idea how it's supposed to feel when you meet *the one*. Then, that day, when I pulled you out of the riverbank, I finally got it. Lightning. Fireworks. Annihilation."

I raise an eyebrow. "Still, you rejected me."

"No, Savannah." His voice cracks. "I'm so sorry I made you feel like that. I was never going to let you go. But I thought holding back, not mating you was the right thing to do. I didn't understand that was exactly what was turning my animal feral again. This is what I've figured out—after these crazy days in the forest—" He draws my hand against his chest and I feel his big heart beating, strong and slow beneath his massive ribcage. "With you, my animal is calm. In harmony with yours. You're my mate, and it's no longer my enemy."

I close my eyes, feeling dizzy and overwhelmed. "But will you be mine and only mine?" I say, in a trembling voice.

He frowns. "What do you mean, Savannah?"

"I don't want to be part of a harem."

"W-what?" He laughs. "There's not gonna be a harem. Where did you get that idea?"

"My pack." I swallow hard. "All the alphas have a harem."

He works his jaw back and forth, then shakes his head as if the thought is abhorrent to him. "Well, not this one. You're mine and I'm yours. And that's all there is. I want you all to myself." His frown gets even deeper. "But you better understand what that means."

I shake my head questioningly.

"I'm a possessive wolf—

I'll barely let you out of my sight—

I'll probably want to know where you're going at all times—

Who you're hanging out with—

Hell, I'll probably vet them first, make sure they're worthy company for you—

I might get bossy and demanding at times—

Yup. Especially, demanding."

As each sentence growls from his lips, shivers run through me, and a deep ache starts up in my core. It's delicious. I probably shouldn't admit that to myself, but there it is. I absolutely love the idea of Beau protecting me. Being all bossy and growly and possessive.

"Maybe that'll be too much," he says.

It sounds like a question, but I see from the way his eyes are burning that he *knows*. He knows this is what I need from my mate.

"Not too much," I say, and I lift my arms up, loop them around his neck.

"It's because I'm besotted with you," he growls, pressing his lips to my forehead.

"You are?" My heart bounds like a rabbit. A little bit of me still can't believe this incredible, smart, sexy man feels like this about me.

"Totally fixated." He dips his head so his eyes are

blazing right into mine. "I love you, Little One. You know that, right?"

I give a little gasp. "No?"

"Of course. I've loved you for a long time."

A grin tugs at my lips. "Then tell me."

He grins. "I love you, Savannah. With all my heart."

"Oh, I love you, too, Beau."

We kiss, and kiss again, thrills chasing through me.

At last, he takes a step back and takes me in. And I let him look, let him get his fill of me. Knowing he sees me as a sexy, desirable woman.

"I'm going to mate you, claim you like I should have done days ago," he growls. His gaze draws a trail of fire with it, instantly hardening my nipples, making a pulse beat between my thighs.

"Is that right?" I say nonchalantly, feeling myself begin to get wet. I still fear the sounds of mating I heard at my pack's territory. But my desire for Beau is stronger than my fear.

He runs his hands over my body—my waist, my arms, my breasts—and unleashes a groan of pure need. "You don't know what you do to me," he mutters. "How hard it's been to hold back all of these days."

"Then show me," I say.

He takes my hand and leads me through the forest. Anticipation surges in me. I can't tear my eyes from his magnificent body. From his big, thick cock which juts out with his desire for me.

11

Savannah

*F*inally, we arrive at the parking lot, Bertha is waiting as patiently as ever. It's still early, and we're the only people there, thank goodness. We step into the back, look at each other, our bodies trembling with an identical need.

"Not here. Let's go home," he says.

I grin, knowing what he means. This is home. But so is the crumbling old parking lot with the river running alongside it. He rummages in a cupboard, finds a T-shirt and shorts and pulls them on, while I slip into my T-shirt, my panties, reach for my jeans.

But he stops me. "That's enough," he growls.

He wants me to sit in the passenger seat in just my panties? *Okay then.*

"What about your bike?" I ask as we take our seats. "Don't you want to ride it back?"

"I'll pick it up later." He gives me another burning look. "There's no way I'm letting you out of my sight right now."

A shiver of delight goes through me.

I'm his. I'm really his, I keep telling myself.

THE RAIN HAS CLEARED NOW and the morning sunshine is brilliant as we drive back to Perdue Town. Beau asks me about the last couple of days. Where I learned to drive a bus. I sense he's keeping the conversation light. There's a lot to talk about, but now is not the time.

Now is the time to satisfy our burning need for each other.

As he drives, his big hand rests on my thigh. Affectionate at first, then riding higher, higher.

"Spread those sweet thighs for me," he murmurs.

I comply eagerly, and his hand slides up, up until he's cupping my pussy through my panties. As he strokes the flimsy fabric with light fingertips, I moan in anticipation.

A little growl escapes his throat. "Tell me what you want, honey," he says. "Tell me what you need."

"I need you right here," I manage to say.

"Then move those panties out of the way."

I do as he says, yanking the fabric aside, exposing myself for him. He drags his eyes away from the road and takes me in. "So pretty, baby. So perfect," he says.

He presses his hand against my bare pussy. I'm

drenched, and his touch on my aching clit is electric. He's a master at teasing me. He spreads my labia, caresses me with featherlight strokes, presses a fingertip just at my entrance before pulling away again. I close my eyes, tip my head back and give in to the sighs and moans spilling from my lips.

"You're so wet for me, baby," he croons. "Does my baby want my cock?"

"Yes," I say, because it's all I can think about right now. That big, thick cock of his, filling me up. "I want you to take my virginity," I say. I hear his breath catching, and it's the sexiest thing I can imagine.

"Yes, that's right little wolf. I'm going to take your virginity. Make you mine," he says. When I open my eyes, I see his cock has tented his pants, and there's a damp spot from his pre-cum. If we're not home in minutes, I'm gonna make him pull over on the side of the road and I'll jump right in his lap.

Several long, agonizing minutes pass. He keeps touching me, driving my arousal, pushing me to the point where I spasm around his fingertip, then drawing back. Playing my body like I'm he's a virtuoso and I'm a violin.

Finally, the river appears, a streak of pure gold on the right-hand side of the road, then the parking lot. Our little piece of paradise.

As he pulls into the usual spot beside the motorcycle trailer, my heart hammers in my chest. The tension in the air is thick. Finally, this moment I've longed for, for days is here.

There's something different in his eyes now, something wild and unfettered, and I know he won't hold back this time. My heart thrills with it.

He jumps out of the bus. "Wait right there," he says, and disappears into the interior.

He's gone for a few minutes, and I force myself not to turn my head and see what he's up to.

At last, he's back. He opens my door and catches me up in his arms.

Then he carries me into the back of the bus.

All the mess my wolf created has been swept away, and somehow a whole double bed has been pulled out from the wall, filling the entire floor space. There's a comforter, two pillows. All downy white and virginal.

Beau lays me down gently and he climbs on top of me, his powerful body curving around me.

My heart beats hard. "You'll be my first," I say.

"And you, mine," he growls in my ear.

He runs his hand over the curve of my belly. But when he reaches beneath the waistband of my panties, I stop him.

"I'm ready for you," I tell him. "I just want your cock. Nothing else."

"Are you sure, little virgin?"

"Very." I sit up and strip off my T-shirt and my panties. Then, while I hold his burning gaze, I spread my legs for him.

A raw sound of need escapes his throat. He tears off his own clothes, and his cock springs out, bigger than ever.

The world stops moving as he presses his cock to my dripping wet entrance. "I'm yours, you're mine." His voice is low, vibrating, close to my ear. "Your first, your last. Your mate, who will always protect you, put you first."

It's like an incantation, wrapping me up in dizzying tendrils of need, longing, love.

And the burn as he pushes through my maidenhead feels like nothing compared to the rush of pleasure that follows it. Tears spring to my eyes, and he kisses them away.

I cling to him tight, overwhelmed by the tingles running through me. Little spasms growing into earth-shattering tremors.

"It didn't really hurt," I manage to say.

He laughs tenderly. "Of course not." He strokes my face. "I told you it would be nothing like that."

"I know, I'm sorry—" I give a little gasp as more of him enters me.

"Easy, honey," he growls. "No rush."

He goes slow, caring for me, as his huge cock takes my virginity. I feel his muscles trembling, sense him holding back with everything he's got.

My thighs are tense, but suddenly I let go, and he pushes all the way into me, with a deep, vibrating growl.

I give a wild cry as he fills me all the way up. My pussy throbs, burns as I yield to his massive girth. Forcing me wide open. It hurts, but it hurts so good.

I cling to his back, dig my nails in, and he gives a groan of pleasure.

"You feel so good," he grits out. "So tight. Barely any room for my cock."

He works himself in and out of me, gliding on my wetness.

I feel my insides gripping him tight, spasming at the blissful friction that goes on and on.

He pushes my knees up and watches himself sliding in and out of me. He's poised over me, big muscles bunched, eyes full of desire and love mingled together. It's too much. Too much. That sweet, intense, welling sensation comes over me again. Every part of me burns for release.

"Beau, I—" I pant.

"Yeah, that's right, baby, come around my cock for the first time," he growls. "I want to feel your virgin pussy milking me."

He goes a little faster, harder, and it hits me *right there*. I'm falling, falling, stars swirling all the way through me, and then I explode around him, his cock buried deep inside me.

I think I scream, wail. Perhaps my animal unleashes a growl, too. And when I open my eyes again, panting for breath, Beau's burning eyes are staring down at me, watching it all happen.

I laugh a little, embarrassed, but he kisses me, growls, "beautiful," in my ear.

And then he's flipping me, and I'm facedown.

Oh, this is different. Up on my hands and knees. I feel shy like this, and I cringe a little as he runs his hands all over me.

Then, with a growl of desire, his cock slides into me again.

And I forget everything else.

I sense him unleashing himself. He's rougher, thrusting himself deeper into me with every stroke. His hips pound against my ass. It's fierce, wild and I can't get enough of it.

Harder, faster. I bury my face in my hands, aware of nothing but the relentless rhythm of his cock, setting my insides on fire. Tipping me into one orgasm after another.

When I'm helpless, and can't take anymore, he lifts me up, wrapping his arms around my waist, and I feel his teeth grazing the back of my neck.

"I'm going to give you my mark," he growls.

"Yes," I gasp. "I want it, Beau. Give it to me."

He's giving me his claiming mark.

The thought blooms in my mind, flows through my body. I close my eyes, feeling my wolf rising to the surface, bonding with his.

His teeth fix on to the nape of my neck, and he fucks me harder, harder. Then with a roar, he comes, deep inside me. I feel his seed filling me up while my skin throbs from his mark.

I'm his, forever.

I PEER through the window of the bus. We've been talking and napping and snuggling all afternoon. The sun has dropped to the horizon, and the sky is shot through with pink and orange. The river lies in the shadows now, but energy snaps in its darkly sparkling water.

"Will you come to the river with me?" I ask Beau. "There's something I want to do."

He's sprawled out on his back beside me, and there's a softness in his features. A new look of contentment.

He runs a finger up and down the small of my back. "Sure, honey," he says, with no hesitation.

A couple of minutes later, we're creeping across along the riverbank, butt-naked. Kind of risky, I guess, but it's always quiet here.

He dives into the water, slick as a fish, and waits for me. I splash in, less elegantly, but he catches me in his arms. The water is cool and silky. I look up and down the river. There's no one here but us. It feels like there's no one in the whole world.

Beau looks at me expectantly, curiosity twitching in his lips. "What are we doing here, darlin'?"

I wrap my arms around his neck. Then I lift up my legs and wrap them around his waist. It's easy like this, with the water buoying me up. I kiss him, long and deep, tangling my hands in his hair, stroking his beard. When a groan bursts from his throat, I know it's time.

I reach down. His cock is as hard as I hoped. "This." Keeping hold of it, I maneuver myself, and when it touches my entrance, I slide it into me.

"Oh, god," he groans, and he pushes himself inside me. "What are you doing to me, woman?"

I was sore after he took my virginity, but the river's washed it away, and I feel brand new as his cock fills me up again.

"Reborn," I mutter. "You gave me a new life when you dragged me out of the river that day."

Beau's eyes are dazzling blue, his teeth flashing as he grins at me. "I think you're right, honey. We both got reborn here."

He holds me tight as he rocks into me, the water twinkling and chattering all around, and we both come at the same time. Me and my fierce, river god mate.

EPILOGUE

Four months later

Standing on the top rung of a stepladder, I stretch up on tiptoes while I work a screwdriver.

There. The brand-new, number 140 sign is now securely attached to the porch. I lean back to admire my handiwork.

"Steady—" Beau is right behind me, his hand resting on the small of my back. As I climb down the ladder, he guides me, with light fingers on my hips. When I reach the penultimate step, I tumble backward into his arms, and he catches me.

Of course, he does.

I giggle in pure happiness. I'll never tire of that feeling of *trusting* him. Of knowing he's always there to protect me.

Wrapping his arms around my waist, he buries his face in the side of my neck and gives a possessive growl. I shiver in delight, and gaze at the brand-new shop that my amazing mate has created for me.

It's all white gingerbread trimmings on powder-blue clapboard—the exact same shade as Bertha. It looks good enough to eat. Every inch of it worked on with love. The inside is flooded with light, ivory walls and wooden floors, and plenty of space to display my designs.

Above the darker blue front door, a sign reads, *Come a Long Way, Baby.*

I picked the name of the store myself. I was worried Beau would think it was dumb, but he said, "it's perfect. It's you, Savannah."

It's also him—because none of this would've happened without his love and support. And that's why I love it.

Naming the store and attaching the street number has been my sole contribution. The rest is all Beau. For the last two months, he kept his little project a secret. Every day, he took me to dress-making school on the back of his motorcycle, then, he came back to Perdue Town and worked on renovating this little store he'd purchased on Main Street. He took a bunch of photos for me—the little building was real run-down and hadn't been inhabited for years. Now, it's a beautifully restored Victorian boutique.

"Congratulations on your new place, Honey," Beau says.

I twist around in his arms and pull him down for a

kiss. His beard is soft beneath my fingertips and his lips as firm and dreamy as ever. "Thank you, thank you, thank you," I say. I still can't believe it's real. Can't believe I have my own place, stocked with my own designs.

Seven days ago, Beau picked me up from school and parked the motorcycle up a couple of streets away. Then he blindfolded me and led me here. When he finally slipped the blindfold off, it took my poor brain a long while to catch up. He wasn't just showing me a ridiculously pretty little building, which stood out in a street of dark, shuttered stores. It was *mine. My own fashion boutique.* Created by my mate, just for me. I burst into tears right there. So much love. So much care for my happiness and dreams.

Ever since then, my head has been bursting with ideas. I have a half-dozen prototype dresses ready. I just signed a contract with a local family-owned factory that will manufacture them for me. And while I'm growing my collection, I'll display the stock of other local designers. Beau is a whiz with the Internet, of course, and he's already helped me track down some contacts.

We take a bunch of photos of the shop and each other. Beau always has his camera out. *Every moment is precious*, he says.

I lock the door, with my brand-new key, then we go pick up Bertha. We're throwing an opening party tomorrow, and we need to go buy some supplies.

All these months later, Bertha is still our home—as well as our transport. Beau has offered to buy me *any mansion, castle or palace I want, in the whole wide world.*

But it turns out, nothing makes us happier than living in our little bus. In time—and definitely when we have cubs—we'll need someplace bigger. But for now, sleeping in this little home, with the river tinkling beside us, is all we need.

* * *

THE FOLLOWING EVENING, I stand in the doorway of my very own boutique, nervously waiting for people to arrive. I put a few signs around town, inviting anybody who wants to come. I also went around and invited all the other businesses on Main Street. Some people were kinda suspicious, a few were even hostile—as people often are in Perdue Town. I'm hoping they'll come around in time, though.

When two tall, statuesque figures appear on the porch, my heart leaps, and I rush out and greet Meredith and her sister, Valeria.

"Told you he was a keeper," Meredith comments, taking in the building with her shrewd gaze.

"You like it?" I'm fishing for compliments, but I don't care. I'm so proud of Beau's work.

"It's…beautiful. Real beautiful," she replies, unusually effusively. "He's done good, that man of yours."

"He has," I say happily.

"And you deserve it, hun. All of it." She sweeps me up in one of her fierce hugs.

My eyes prickle and I blink back tears. "Thank you," I manage to say. I don't work at Sinner's anymore—when I'm not busy with school assignments, Beau demands all my time—but my relationship with Meredith has continued to grow. She's truly the mother I never had.

Right after Beau claimed me, he tracked down my pack. Then he asked me if I wanted to visit them, demand to know who my real mom was. With no hesitation, I said no. It doesn't matter to me anymore. Beau's love fills my heart completely. When I need advice on girl stuff, and mothering, Meredith's there for me. And when Elinor and I are both free at the same time, we hang out, gossiping and watching movies. My whole life is here now, with this little 'found family' of mine. And I feel like the luckiest girl in the world.

"It's a lovely place, dear," Valeria adds. "I think you'll be very happy and successful."

I hug her too, then I show them inside and offer a plate of the cookies I baked in Sinner's kitchen yesterday.

After that, it gets busy. Turns out all the suspicious folk are also real curious, and plenty of familiar faces from the town shuffle in and poke around the store.

"If you're not careful, you might create some community spirit here," Beau growls in my ear, wrapping an arm around my waist.

I grin. "Imagine that, in Perdue—" Then I frown. "That's a good thing, right?"

"Of course. It's always gonna be a place where people can come hide from the world if they want. But a little community spirit will make it safer for everyone."

Elinor arrives after her shift at Sinner's, accompanied by a bunch of girls from the dorm.

"This is fricking fantastic, Sav!" she exclaims, and the *oohs* and *ahhs* from the other girls makes me smile. I'm already planning to donate some sets of clothes to the waifs and strays who arrive at Sinner's with nothing more than the clothes on their backs.

As more and more people arrive, my eyes keep darting to the door. I'm awaiting two special guests, and the thought fills me with a mixture of nerves and excitement.

At last, two strangers emerge from the twilight. They stand on the porch, taking everything in. I've never seen them before in my life, yet I think I'd recognize them anywhere.

Tall, broad-shouldered, with glowing, cornflower-blue eyes.

My stomach fizzing, I turn and look for Beau.

There he is, helping an old lady to a cup of soda. The second he's done, I grab his hand and haul him to the front door.

"Where's the fire?" he exclaims, laughing. Then he skids to a stop, his breath catching. I feel the vibrations from his heartbeat as if they're my own.

"Luke? Mason?" he says at last.

Both men have hard, angular features with a hostile cast, but when the taller of the two smiles, his face transforms.

"Hello, big brother," he says.

Beau exhales a long breath, takes a step forward, and they're hugging. Rough, back-slapping man hugs.

I watch, tears springing to my eyes as Beau and his two younger brothers are reunited. Then they're talking non-stop, catching up on the years. I'm content to stand back and watch it happen.

"You shouldn't have stayed away, bro," Luke—the taller one—says. "We missed you, *so* fucking much."

"I had to. It's long story," Beau replies. "I was in a bad place, for a long time. But now I'm healed." He reaches for me, draws me into the circle.

"I'm guessing you've already been introduced to my beautiful mate?"

"Not in person," Mason says, shaking my hand. He's more standoffish than Luke, with a searing, almost feral stare, but I can tell he's happy to see his brother again.

Leaving them to catch up, I return to the guests, my heart glowing. I was so nervous that something would go wrong, that they wouldn't make it in time, but it all turned out better than I hoped.

The guys hang out with Beau for an hour or so, then they head to their motel, making plans to catch up tomorrow. I tell Beau it's fine for him to leave and hang out with them.

"Nope. No way am I leaving you alone on your special night," he tells me. "There'll be plenty of time to hang out in future."

A little thrill goes through me—as I have one more surprise planned for Beau tonight.

"Just tell me one thing," he says, shaking his head. "How did you track them down?"

"You're not the only investigator in town, you

know?" I wrap my arms around his firm waist. "I might've used your equipment to run a few searches."

He grins and plants kisses on my forehead. "My smart, beautiful, amazing mate."

"Are you happy I did this?" I ask, a dart of uncertainty hitting me.

"Yup. Very. It's time," he says, and I pick up the many shades of emotion in his voice.

* * *

IT'S GONE eleven by the time the last guests tumble out of the door of my little boutique.

"Whew." Beau locks the door behind us. "Some folks *really* had a good time tonight."

"Knew we shouldn't have given them wine."

We look at each other, laughing.

Then he takes my hands in his. "I think you brought something real special into people's lives."

"I did?" My heart is glowing. I've got twenty-one new orders in my order book, and people kept asking about my plans for a made-to-measure range—designed to cater for curvy girls, big bear shifters, and everyone in between.

When I loop my arms around his neck, he lifts me by my waist and spins me around. I love the way he makes me feel so small and delicate in his big arms.

He looks around at the remains of the party. "Shall we close up now and deal with all this tomorrow?" he suggests.

I bite my lip, excitement fizzing in my stomach. "Yes, but I have one design I haven't showed you yet."

His eyes light up immediately. "Show me," he says. And I glow a little bit more. I love the way that he's not just supportive of my passion, but actively excited, always demanding I show him what I'm working on.

I position a chair in the middle of the shop floor and ask him to take a seat.

With a slightly bemused expression, he complies, and as I run around the store, closing all the drapes, I feel his curious eyes burning into me. Then I turn the lights right down, until a single spotlight is focused on the floor six feet or so in front of him.

"Close your eyes, and don't move a muscle," I say. My mouth is a little dry. I'm not used to bossing my big, dominant alpha mate around.

He throws me a good-natured smirk, acknowledging the fact.

Then I dash to the storeroom at the rear of the shop.

WHEN I RETURN five minutes later, I ignore a slight prickle of nerves and hold my head high, put my shoulders back, and focus on walking confidently in my sky-high stilettoes. I have a mate who loves me; who tells me every day that I'm the sexiest woman in the world, and the knowledge fills me with confidence.

I watch Beau as I approach, wondering if he really kept his eyes shut. But there's no hint of that burning-sky blue between his eyelashes.

I stop right under the spotlight, trembling with anticipation.

"Open them," I say.

He opens his eyes, and his jaw drops. Literally.

"Wow," he breathes.

As his gaze rakes me up and down, the raw passion on his face fires my own desire.

"Like it?"

"Uh huh," he growls, and I see his cock is already hardening beneath the zipper of his jeans.

Being desired by this big, sexy guy is intoxicating. I never in a million years imagined I'd the kind of girl who'd flirt like this. But right now, I feel like a goddess.

"Turn around," he growls, making a circling motion with his finger.

So, I do. I circle around slowly, treating him to a full three-sixty.

"You made them," he says, in a hoarse voice.

I break into a smile. "I did."

The lace-top stockings I bought from a store, but the bra, slip, panties and garter belt I made myself, in cherry-red lace and satin.

"It's a prototype, but I think it turned out pretty well."

His Adam's apple bobs and he licks his lips. "You can say that again." He slaps his hands down on his knees. "C'mere."

I sashay over to him, basking in his attention. Arousal swirls through me, turning my nipples to hard, little pebbles and lighting a fire between my thighs. I lay my hands on his shoulders, and let my hair fall into his face while I wiggle my hips, just a little bit.

He groans and his hands land on my ass cheeks with a resounding slap. "Beautiful," he growls. He draws me closer, and I straddle his lap until I'm sitting down, my aching clit riding his cock. Beau runs his hands all over the satin and lace, sounds of pleasure escaping his lips.

My concept is for a whole range of lingerie for curvy girls, that has a soft, luxurious look and feel. And by his reaction, I've succeeded.

"Think they've been on for long enough, though," he says. He slides the silky slip over my head, then he unclips my bra. The panties have naughty little ties at the sides—because I designed them with sex in mind. He unfastens them with deft fingers and they fall away. And there I am, naked on his lap, in just a garter belt, stockings and spike heels.

"Wish you could see how sexy you look right now," he mutters, his eyes burning with yearning.

"I can see you, and that's all I need," I whisper. I tug on his shirt, dragging it up and off, and then I reach for his zipper. While he's busy worshipping my breasts, I guide his rock-hard cock inside me. And as I ride my incredible mate to heaven, I know I'll never forget this moment.

THE END

READ THE OTHER BOOKS IN THE SERIES

If you like steamy insta-love romance, featuring obsessed, growly heroes who'll do anything for their mates, check out the rest of the books in my Obsessed Mates series. All books are standalone and can be read in any order.

Continue the series at arianahawkes.com/obsessed-mates

READ MY OBSESSED MOUNTAIN MATES SERIES

If you like fated-mate romances, with plenty of V-card fun and tons of feels, check out my Obsessed Mountain Mates series. All books are standalone and can be read in any order.

Get started at arianahawkes.com/obsessed-mountain-mates

READ THE REST OF MY CATALOGUE

MateMatch Outcasts: a matchmaking agency for beasts, and the women tough enough to love them.

★★★★★ "A super **exciting, funny, thrilling, suspenseful and steamy shifter romance series**. The characters jump right off the page!"

★★★★★ "**Absolutely Freaking Fantastic**. I loved every single word of this story. It is so full of **exciting twists that will keep you guessing until the very end** of this book. I can't wait to see what might happen next in this series."

Ragtown is a small former ghost town in the mountains, populated by outcast shifters. It's a secretive place, closed-off to the outside world - until someone sets up a secret mail-order bride service that introduces women looking for their mates.

Get started at arianahawkes.com/matematch-outcasts

MY OTHER MATCHMAKING SERIES

My bestselling *Shiftr: Swipe Left For Love* series features Shiftr, the secret dating app that brings curvy girls and sexy shifters their perfect match! Fifteen books of totally bingeworthy reading — and my readers tell me that Shiftr is their favorite app ever! ;-) Get started at arianahawkes. com/shiftr

★★★★★ "**Shiftr is one of my all-time favorite series**! The stories are funny, sweet, exciting, and scorching hot! And they will **keep you glued to the pages**!"

★★★★★ "**I wish I had access to this app**! Come on, someone download it for me!"

Get started at arianahawkes.com/shiftr

CONNECT WITH ME

If you'd like to be notified about new releases, giveaways and special promotions, you can sign up to my mailing list at arianahawkes.com/mailinglist. You can also follow me on BookBub and Amazon at:

bookbub.com/authors/ariana-hawkes
amazon.com/author/arianahawkes

Thanks again for reading – and for all your support!

Yours,
Ariana

* * *

USA Today bestselling author Ariana Hawkes writes spicy romantic stories with lovable characters, plenty of suspense, and a whole lot of laughs. She told her first story at the age of four, and has been writing ever since, for both work and pleasure. She lives in Massachusetts with her husband and two huskies.

www.arianahawkes.com

GET TWO FREE BOOKS

Join my mailing list and get two free books.

 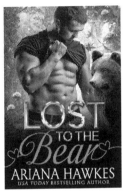

Once Bitten Twice Smitten

A 4.5-star rated, comedy romance featuring one kickass roller derby chick, two scorching-hot Alphas, and the naughty nip that changed their lives forever.

Lost To The Bear

He can't remember who he is. Until he meets the woman he'll never forget.

Get your free books at arianahawkes.com/freebook

READING GUIDE TO ALL OF MY BOOKS

Obsessed Mates

Her River God Wolf

Her Biker Wolf

Her Alpha Neighbor Wolf

Her Bad Boy Trucker Wolf

Her Second Chance Wolf

Her Convict Wolf

Obsessed Mountain Mates

Driven Wild By The Grizzly

Snowed In With The Grizzly

Chosen By The Grizzly

Off-Limits To The Grizzly

Shifter Dating App Romances

Shiftr: Swipe Left for Love 1: Lauren

Shiftr: Swipe Left for Love 2: Dina

Shiftr: Swipe Left for Love 3: Kristin

Shiftr: Swipe Left for Love 4: Melissa

Shiftr: Swipe Left for Love 5: Andrea

Shiftr: Swipe Left for Love 6: Lori

Shiftr: Swipe Left for Love 7: Adaira

Shiftr: Swipe Left for Love 8: Timo

Shiftr: Swipe Left for Love 9: Jessica

Shiftr: Swipe Left for Love 10: Ryzard

Shiftr: Swipe Left for Love 11: Nash

Shiftr: Swipe Left for Love 12: Olsen

Shiftr: Swipe Left for Love 13: Frankie

Shiftr: Swipe Left for Love 14: Niall

Shiftr: Swipe Left for Love 15: Dalton

MateMatch Outcasts

Grizzly Mate

Protector Mate

Rebel Mate

Monster Mate

Dragon Mate

Wild Mate

In Dragn Protection

Ethereal King

Boreas Reborn

Wounded Wings

Broken Hill Bears

Bear In The Rough

Bare Knuckle Bear

Bear Cuffs

Standalone releases

Tiger's Territory

Shifter Holiday Romances

Bear My Holiday Hero

Ultimate Bear Christmas Magic Boxed Set Vol. 1

Ultimate Bear Christmas Magic Boxed Set Vol. 2

Made in the USA
Columbia, SC
06 March 2025

54741161R00087